10

ISBN-13: **978-1544793863**

Published in the United States of America
Edited by Diane Shirk

Calaway Jones

A Harry Starke Novel

By

Blair Howard

For Jo

Thank you for your patience, my love.

Chapter 1
Saturday, June 17
United States Penitentiary, Atlanta

Gordon Harper was seated on his bed in his cell staring at the screen on his iPad—a perk he'd paid dearly for. He'd already watched the video a half dozen times, but he couldn't tear himself away from it.

It was an item from yesterday's Channel 7 early evening newscast that his lackey Lester "Shady" Tree had e-mailed to him about an hour earlier. Harper was doing a twenty-five-year stretch for a litany of crimes from tax evasion to conspiracy to commit murder. *And all because of that smug son of a bitch,* he thought, as he started the video over again.

"So, Mr. Starke," the interviewer said, shoving his microphone into Starke's face. "You did it again. You've put away another bad guy—well, gal in this case. How do you feel about that?"

What a stupid friggin' question, Harper thought, grinding his teeth.

Starke hesitated, then said, "I feel... both good... and sickened, if you want to know the truth." *The truth! The truth is that son of a bitch Starke killed my daughter!* Harper thought.

It had been back in early 2015 when Harry had brought him down, him and several of his inner circle, but not Shady Tree. Harper trusted Tree, as far as he trusted anybody, although he sometimes wondered if the man was playing with a full deck. Tree and his two lieutenants, Duvon James and Henry Gold, had gotten away when Harper was brought to justice, although James had been injured and Gold had died during a shootout with Starke a little more than a year later.

Henry Gold he couldn't care less about, but Starke had also killed Harper's daughter, Kathryn, and her husband, Jonathan Greene. He'd never gotten over that.

As for Duvon James, he had recovered from injuries received in that same altercation and had somehow managed to cut a deal that put him back on the streets less than a year later. Now he and Tree were together again, and a more depraved pair would have been hard to find—and both were on Harper's payroll. It didn't give him his daughter back, but it was something.

"You say you're sickened," the interviewer said, "but Mary Ann Warren killed two people in cold blood, one of them her husband, the other… well, we won't go into details, they're too graphic, but sickened? I would have thought you'd have been feeling… *elated*."

Starke's eyebrows raised as he grimaced; the interviewer was a small man, dwarfed by Starke's height.

"Charlie... you might think that, and maybe you're right; Mrs. Warren was a stone-cold killer, and Peter Nicholson was only thirty-three when she killed him. Think of all that wasted potential. What great things might he have accomplished, had he lived? And his mother, Helen... Charlie, she didn't deserve... she... I don't think I've ever seen a more brutal, more... callous killing. And then there's Mary Ann herself. What kind of mind loads up a truck with concrete blocks and then drives it back and forth over a fellow human being? Yes, Charlie, I feel sickened."

Charlie Grove nodded seriously, playing to the camera. "What put you onto Mary Ann, Harry? From what I've read about the case it could have been... well, I understand you had Judge Warren in your sights, until..."

Starke nodded. "Look, there were a whole lot more people than just me involved. The Chattanooga PD, Lieutenant Gazzara—" he turned to look at her, "—Mike Willis, Joanne Snyder, not to mention the medical examiner, Doc Sheddon. And there was my own team: Jacque Hale—that's her there—Ronnie Hall, and Tim Clarke, especially Tim. Hell, Charlie, even you had a finger in the pie. It really was a team effort. In the end, though, it was the science, the forensics, that put her away."

Grove grinned up at him, obviously pleased at the mention. "But it was you who figured it out, right? I understand about the science, but someone had to interpret it, and that was you, Harry, just you."

Starke shrugged but didn't reply.

"So," Grove continued, obviously reluctant to turn loose the spotlight, "you recently got married, and to Channel 7's own Amanda Cole, no less. My congratulations to both of you. No one saw that coming either." He turned and smiled at the statuesque blonde woman standing just behind him. She tilted her head slightly and smiled at him.

"Any comments about that, Harry?"

"Er… no!"

"Oh come on. Look at her. Surely a word…"

"They don't call you Pitbull for nothing, do they, Charlie? No, not even a word. Now, if you don't mind." He turned away from Grove and the camera, took the blonde woman's hand, and walked down the steps to a waiting car.

Harper dropped the iPad onto the bed, laced his fingers behind his neck, leaned back against the cell wall, closed his eyes, and was soon lost in thought.

Arrogant son of a bitch. Piece o' garbage. Damn… I hate that smug bastard. I'm gonna get

4

him, by God. I am... I am... Piece of shit! I'm gonna kill him. Kathryn... my little girl. Jon... friggin' idiot... Kathryn.

Involuntarily, he shook his head. He wasn't a sentimental man, but he loved his children: he'd had three girls. Kathryn had been the middle child and his favorite. She'd taken over the running of his vast, albeit corrupt, financial empire when he went inside. Jordan, his eldest, was a professor of economics at Georgia Tech; Lexi his youngest, as yet unmarried, was now in charge of all that Little Billy Harper had once surveyed and, to his amazement and delight, was even better at it than Kathryn had been. Unfortunately, the girl, unlike Kathryn, was honest so there would be no help there. At least not the kind he was looking for.

Harper was now sixty-five. He didn't feel sorry for himself, but he did tend to live in the past, remembering, reliving the glory days when he had the world in the palm of his hand. Back when lesser men—and that meant almost everyone he'd ever come in contact with—bowed to his will, and when he was one of the three most powerful men in the United States Congress.

But those days were long gone. He would be eighty-eight when he got out of USP Atlanta if he lived that long. Incarcerated? Yes. Powerless? No. He was the uncrowned king of not just his own medium security cell block, but the entire complex. His reach extended into every corner, to every one of the 2,268 other inmates, and to many of the guards and administrators. He was respected as the "power inside." His vast wealth, although largely unavailable to him, could still be relied upon to buy the "necessities," and it was those perks and privileges that made life, even inside, almost bearable. It was easy enough. A simple call to Shady, cash changed hands, and he got what he wanted.

Over the past several weeks... no, over the years since he'd been put away, but more so recently, he'd been thinking about all he'd lost at the hands of Harry Starke, especially Kathryn. The more he thought about Starke, the more the hate gnawed at his insides. Long ago, Harper had known he was going to have Starke killed. Had he done so during the first months of his incarceration, it would have been enough. Now, more than two years on, and following one success of Starke's after another, it wasn't. The man had to hurt; he had to suffer; he had to lose, as Harper had lost, all those things most dear to him.

Harper sat up, reached for the iPad, flipped the screen, entered his code, and ran the video again.

And we'll start with the blonde bitch, Amanda Cole... Amanda Starke. That should hurt some. And then what? Who? Who can I... Maybe... Hmmm. I wonder... If anyone could pull it off, she could. Where is she, I wonder? I need to find out. Well, I need someone to find out for me... not

Lexi… He sighed, shook his head, set the iPad down and picked up his iPhone from the top of the small nightstand—another one of his perks bought and paid for at great cost.

He punched in the number from memory. It wasn't smart to store numbers in the phone; a man could get into trouble that way. And then he waited, the phone to his ear. Shady answered on the second ring.

"Hey, Boss. How's it?"

"I need to see you. Today. Get your ass down here," he said and disconnected before Tree could answer or refuse.

***

Not that Shady ever would refuse. He valued his health, and his life, too much for that, but he did scowl and look at his watch.

"Shit, it be after 'leven. Damn, damn, damn," he said to himself. "Best ge' m'self gone."

Only when he was alone did Shady revert to his own personal style of Ebonics. It was a fun thing and a reminder of his roots. When in public, however, his accent was almost refined. He dressed well, too. His signature gray suits were handmade, as were his snakeskin loafers. He liked to look good. He liked to impress. Even his dreads were neat and shiny.

He left the house on North Chamberlain, eased himself into his midnight blue BMW M6, hit the starter, turned up the radio, reversed out onto the road, and headed north toward Highway 153. Ten minutes later he was on I-75 heading toward the Split. Ninety minutes later, at just after two o'clock in the afternoon, he was parked in the lot outside the prison on McDonough Boulevard in Atlanta.

He walked through the main entrance, waited patiently, and then endured the bullshit security checks until, with only a few minutes left of visiting hours, he found himself in the visiting area, seated at a table across from his boss, Little Billy Harper.

"How are you doing, sir?" he asked. It was part of their weekly ritual: he asked all the stupid questions, and Harper provided all the stock answers. They had been doing it once a week for more than a year. This time, however, the visit was unscheduled and Harper seemed in no mood for trivialities.

"I'm good. I need you to do something for me." He looked around at the guard standing by the window, watching them. He held up a small envelope for the guard and the cameras to see and tilted his head in question. The guard nodded imperceptibly, and Harper handed it to Tree.

Harper lowered his head so that the cameras couldn't see his lips, and said, "Don't open that until you get out of here. Don't speak. Don't ask questions. I won't answer them. You hear?"

Tree folded the envelope once and slipped it into the inside pocket of his suit jacket. "Yes sir."

"Good," Harper said, still looking down at the table. "There's a note for you inside, and another envelope. Everything you need to know is written down in the note. Read it. Digest it. Then burn it. Talk to no one except her. You got that?"

"Got it."

Harper nodded, looked up at him, and smiled. "Excellent. And how are things in Chattanooga?" he asked, his voice now normal.

Tree looked a little confused, "Fine… I guess. Why?"

"Have you seen Lexi?"

"Last Thursday, like always… Mr. Harper—"

"That's *Congressman*," he snapped. Then he smiled and licked his lips, "Well, how is she?"

Tree shuddered. Harper scared the crap out of him.

"She's fine, sir. I'm keeping an eye on her, just like you asked."

"Good." Harper lowered his head again and, his lips barely moving, whispered, "We can't discuss anything. We're being recorded—sound and video. Don't say anything. Take the envelope and go. If they stop you and ask to see it we're screwed, but they won't. I paid 'em off, big time.

Follow the instructions in the envelope. We'll forgo the weekly meetings for a while. We can talk on the phone until this is done. Don't call me. I'll call you. You answer my questions; say as little as possible, just yes and no. No names, no details. You do what I ask, we're good, and I'll see you right. Understand? Now get the hell out of here and call me in two days."

Ten minutes later, Shady Tree was back in his BMW and trying to beat the traffic; rush hour in Atlanta was already under way, and it wasn't yet three o'clock. It took him more than an hour to get through Marietta where the traffic lessened to a mere torrent, but by then his curiosity was driving him crazy.

He burned through the I-75/I-575 split and then took the Chastain Road exit into Kennesaw. From there he drove two blocks north and swung the Beemer into the Starbucks lot. He turned off the motor, reached into his pocket for the envelope, took out the single sheet of paper inside, and read the fifteen words written on it.

Calaway Jones? Who the hell is that?

Chapter 2
One Day Earlier, Friday, June 16
Hamilton County Courthouse

We were standing in a group on the steps of the courthouse facing cameras and reporters from all four local news channels, and several more from the print press. What was it Andy Warhol said? Something like, "In the future, everyone will be world-famous for 15 minutes." Huh! That so-called delicious fifteen minutes of fame. Me? I'd had my fifteen minutes, many times over. The Nicholson case being only the latest in almost a dozen that had put me under the national spotlight. I was kinda getting used to it, but I didn't like it. Fame, so I've found, has a way of biting you in the ass.

Be that as it may, there we were. Me being interviewed for Channel 7 by Pitbull Charlie Grove and most of the folks involved in bringing Mary Ann to trial were there too: my good friend and one-time, now some-time, partner, Lieutenant Kate Gazzara; Assistant District Attorney Larry Spruce who'd handled the case for the prosecution; my beautiful wife of eight months, Amanda, herself a lead anchor at Channel 7; the various members of my crew, headed by my Personal Assistant, Jacque Hale.

Mary Ann Warren's trial had begun at nine o'clock on Monday morning June 5 with jury selection and had ended with the verdict and sentencing on Friday two weeks later. She was found guilty of the first-degree murder of Helen Nicholson and sent to prison for life without the possibility of parole. From what ADA Larry Spruce had said, the state wouldn't bother to try her for the murder of Peter Nicholson, not unless she won the inevitable appeal, preferring instead to save the state the expense.

The investigation had left me drained. Amanda and I had been married for less than two months the day Helen had walked into my office and asked me to look into her son's death more than fifteen years earlier. Little did I know then that less than three weeks later she herself would be brutally murdered. Now, not quite six months later, it was over, and I had brought their killer to justice. It was bittersweet. Mary Ann Warren was going away for life, but Helen would never know...

It should have been a time for celebration, and no doubt we'd do a little of that later. For now, however, all I wanted to do was get the hell away from the cameras in general and Pitbull Charlie in particular, especially when he decided to bring up my recent marriage to Amanda.

I could have slapped him. I'd known him for a number of years, but our friendship, tenuous as it was, had begun with the Nicholson case when I'd been foolish enough to agree to an exclusive in return for his help. The help had been forthcoming and in return, so had the exclusive. Now he was milking it for all it was worth.

I decided the interview was over, turned away from him, grabbed Amanda's hand, and led her down the steps to the meter where I'd parked my car. I needed to get the hell away from there.

I put the car in gear and headed north on Market Street toward the bridge. I had no idea where I was going, just… somewhere. I turned right on Fourth and then headed out onto Riverside, then Amnicola, past the Police Department, turned right onto 153 and finally onto I-75 heading south toward Dalton. How it happened, I have no idea but, finally, we ended up in the parking lot at the Filling Station. It wasn't the first time, and it for sure wouldn't be the last; their fried chicken is… well, it's really good.

The ride had been a fairly quick one. My mood that day was not one for observing the speed limits. Luckily, though, I made it without being stopped, much to Amanda's relief. She'd said little during the ride; she knows me well enough to let me brood when I need to, but the minute we sat down, even before we ordered, she started in on me.

No, she's not a nag, but she does like to get her point across, usually quite gently… It was also at that point I spotted a couple of women seated by the window across from us. They were staring at us, at Amanda, and were whispering together. Inwardly, I sighed.

There was no getting away from it, even here, in Dalton, on the very edge of the Chattanooga TV market area. Amanda is a well-known and popular personality, but it's more than that: she stands out in a crowd.

A strikingly beautiful woman in her mid-thirties, she's a tall, strawberry blonde, with a figure that's as close to perfect as you can get. She wears her hair cut short, elfin-like, so that it frames her heart-shaped face. The high, prominent cheekbones give her a classic beauty; her small, slightly upturned nose adds cute to the mix, but it is her eyes that define her: wide-set, they are the color of pale green jade.

So, between that and her job, it wasn't unusual that she drew attention whenever she stepped into a room; I just wasn't expecting it here. *And here they come…*

"Ms. Cole?" the smaller of the two women asked, hesitantly.

She looked up at them and smiled, "Yes, what can I do for you?"

"Oh, well…" She was already delving into her oversized, and obviously heavy, handbag. "I was wondering if you… and… It's Harry Starke, isn't it? I was wondering if I could get your autographs.

I'm a big fan. I watch you every night... well, not every night, you're not on *every* night, are you, but when you are..." She finally ran out of steam and offered Amanda a grubby envelope.

Amanda continued to smile. She was used to the attention; I wasn't.

"I can do better than that," she said, opening her own Valentino clutch and taking from it a 5x7 headshot of herself. I had to grin. It was all a part of the narcissistic world of the TV personality, although I had to admit that Amanda was always discreet about how she went about it. Anyway, she signed her name at the bottom of the photo and then handed it to the woman, who deftly handed it to me.

"What?" I said.

"You too please, Mr. Starke."

Now that was a first, and a little embarrassing to boot.

"Me? Why me?"

"You're famous too. I'd love to get you both... together."

I almost sighed and rolled my eyes, but I didn't do either. I made nice, gave her my best smile, took the pen from Amanda, scrawled my name under hers, and handed the photo back to the woman. They thanked us and left, twittering together and looking at their prize, back to their table: they never took their eyes off us until the moment they left some ten minutes later.

"Welcome to my world," Amanda said as they walked away. "Now you know what I have to go through."

"Oh hell, Amanda. You love it. You and those other... Those other..."

"Go on. Say it."

"Those other pussies you work with. Does Charlie Grove carry those things around with him too?"

"Oh boy, does he ever? He has the big ones, the 8x10s. So do the rest of the on-air personalities. I prefer the smaller ones. They're easier to carry."

"Wow," I said, shaking my head. "You were going to say something before they interrupted us. What was it?"

She furrowed her brow and wrinkled her nose—too, too cute. "I was? I... Oh, yes. I was going to ask you what was wrong. You were in a foul mood all the way here. Was it Charlie?"

"Yes, it was Charlie. He's insensitive, sleazy, and an idiot."

"Yup, that's Charlie, but you know what, Harry. The public loves him for it. For all his rudeness and lack of couth, he cares, and he has a softer side, and it shows through. He likes you, Harry. He always has, for as long as I've known him. Though why I don't know. Maybe it's a little bit of hero worship… or something…" She smiled as she said it, and winked at me. I ignored her and took a sip of my Blue Moon.

"Oh come on, Harry. You're not on one of those down, blackest of black moods kicks again, are you? If you are, I swear I'll leave you, forever."

"Hah!" I grinned at her. "Fat chance. Where would you go?"

"Ehhh, I know people. I have a cousin, somewhere… in Australia, I think. Better yet, I can use some of my money to buy a nice condo on the riverbank… Do you remember that Harry?" she asked, a little wistfully. "I sometimes miss that condo, and the river, especially the river."

I nodded, "Yeah, me too." And I did miss it, especially on a summer night when the water was quiet, glistening… "Maybe we should… A summer place, maybe. What do you think?"

"It's a thought. It's summer now, well, almost. Shall I look around a little? We could use that realtor who found us our house."

"Couldn't hurt. Might be fun to look. No, Amanda, I'm not in one of my moods. Charlie caught me a little off-guard when he brought you into the picture. I wasn't expecting it, and… well, you know how paranoid I get when it comes to your safety."

"*Harry!* I'm a TV news anchor. I'm always on display."

"True, but you're not always linked to me; that's what I don't like. I have enemies, and what better way to get at me than through you? Yeah, I worry about it. I worry about it a lot, all the time in fact."

She didn't answer. I don't think she knew what to say. I sure as hell didn't. Suddenly, I was all but overcome by a dreadful feeling of impending doom. I shuddered. She saw it, tilted her head and narrowed her eyes.

"What? What are you thinking?"

"Nothing… It was nothing, just one of those, 'somebody just walked over my grave' things." *Or maybe it was your grave.*

Again, she had nothing to say, so we sat together for a few minutes more, mostly in silence, Amanda holding my hand under the table. But I couldn't rid myself of the feeling that… And you know me; some say I have second sight. Whatever, my gut rarely steers me in the wrong direction.

Finally, she squeezed my hand and said, brightly, "Let's go home, Harry. I need to be alone with you."

And we did. And sometime in the middle of the night I awoke, sweating profusely, and in a state of blind panic. I lay there staring up into the dark reaches of the cathedral ceiling, listening to Amanda breathing steadily by my side, until finally I drifted off again into an uneasy sleep.

I awoke early the following morning to bright sunshine beaming into our bedroom through the open drapes, and I felt better, a whole lot better, but I remembered; at least I think I did. I looked over at Amanda sleeping peacefully next to me. What woke me last night...? A dream, perhaps? Maybe... Maybe not!

Chapter 3
Tuesday, July 11, 10:15am

I was in my office going through some case notes when my iPhone buzzed on my desktop; it was Amanda, "Hey you. What's up?"

"Harry," she sounded upset, panicky, "can you come to the station, now?"

I looked at my watch. It was a little after ten o'clock, "I can, but…"

"Good," she interrupted me. "As soon as you can. I'll be waiting. Kate is already on her way," and with that, she disconnected, leaving me staring at the phone, and with an icy feeling in my gut. *Kate is already on her way. What the hell is that about?*

I almost called her back but thought better of it. Instead, I quickly headed out the door leaving Jacque staring after me.

I arrived at Channel 7 ten minutes later to find the place surrounded by police and sheriff's cruisers, blue lights flashing, the parking lot roped off with yellow and black tape, and cops everywhere. Amanda was standing off to one side talking to Kate, Captain Jim Saddler from the sheriff's department and… Sergeant Lonnie Guest, Kate's sometime partner. *What the hell…?*

I parked the Maxima on the street and ducked under the tape only to be stopped by a uniformed officer. I was about to explain when Lonnie shouted for the officer to let me through.

Amanda was as white as a sheet and trembling from head to toe, obviously in shock.

"What the hell has happened?" I asked, grabbing her by the shoulders. "What's going on?"

"That's what we want to know," Guest said.

"Harry," Kate touched my arm. I loosened my grip on Amanda and turned to look at her. "There's been a shooting. No, calm down. No one was hurt, but Amanda was the target... well, sort of. I need you to come and look at her vehicle."

It was then I noticed Amanda's white Lexus RX, a hybrid SUV on the far side of the lot. It too had been taped off.

I let go of Amanda, told her to stay put, and followed Kate and the other officers under the tape.

"Check it out," Kate said, pointing at the driver's side window.

I did, and my blood ran cold. Stuck to the upper right corner of the driver's side window was one of those small, round, black and yellow smiley face stickers. It was maybe three inches in diameter and... it had a bullet hole through it. It was the bullet hole, just a touch left of dead center, that sent chills down my spine. Whoever had made the shot was good, very good.

I peered in through the car window, and I could see that the bullet had passed through the vehicle and exited via the passenger side window.

I turned to Kate, "What the f…?"

She nodded, "That's not all, Harry. This was stuck under the windshield wiper. Gloves please."

I grabbed a pair of latex gloves from the box Lonnie was holding and put them on; she handed me a single sheet of paper, folded once. Amanda's name was written on the outside. I opened it and stared down at it, horrified, at the nine words written on it.

"Stand absolutely still Amanda and you won't get hurt." It was handwritten, the writing beautiful and precise.

"What… what… the hell is this, Kate?" I was barely able to get the words out, I was so shaken.

"That's what we want to know," she replied. "Harry, what the hell have you done?"

"Done? Done? *Done?* What the hell do you mean by that? I haven't done a damn thing. I… I… need to go to Amanda."

I stripped off the gloves and walked the few yards back to where she was standing. *Oh my God; she looks terrible.*

She was standing with her right arm across her waist, her left thumbnail in her mouth, her face

22

was totally devoid of color; she looked like she was dead. I couldn't believe it.

"Jesus Christ, Amanda. Are you okay?" I asked, putting my arm around her shoulder.

She took her thumbnail out of her mouth, reached up, grabbed my hand, and squeezed, hard, "No, Harry. No, I'm not. I'm scared shitless. I felt the wind of it as it passed by my cheek. I'm… I'm… I'm f… I'm terrified is what I am, Harry. That note had my name on it. Why me?"

Oh yeah, she was scared. Never, in all the time I had known her, had she ever uttered a single profanity; this was as close as she'd ever come, and it did more to get my attention than anything else she could have said, but my mind was in turmoil. I couldn't think worth a damn. I didn't know what the hell to say to her. All I could think of; all I could see, running through my head like a goddam slow motion movie, was the bullet hitting the back of her head, her face exploding: blood, flesh, bone, and brain matter flying in every direction. *Shit! I need to sit down.*

"C'mon," I pulled her gently, steering her toward my car, but then I saw Kate holding up her hand.

"Give us a few minutes, Kate. I just want to take her to my car…" And then I noticed the TV camera on the steps of the building. How long it had been there, I didn't know; long enough, I was sure. I had to get her out of there. "I'll be back, okay?"

She nodded, folded her arms, and watched as I opened the passenger side door of the Maxima and helped her into the seat.

I went around the front of the car and got in beside her, put my arm around her, and pulled her close. She wasn't crying, but her breath was coming in short, sharp gasps. She shuddered, turned, put her arms around my neck and laid her head on my chest. I could feel her trembling.

For maybe five minutes, I sat there, holding her, and slowly she began to calm down. Finally, she sat up, pushed me away, took a deep breath, and said, "I'm okay, now, Harry. You need to get back out there. You need to find who did this. You need to get them, Harry. Go on, go. I'll stay here. I'll be all right."

Reluctant as I was to leave her, I knew I had to. She was right. I had to find out who did this.

"Okay, stay put. I'll be... well, I'll get back as soon as I can. Lock the doors and keep 'em locked. Don't open them to anyone but me, and I mean *anyone*."

She nodded, sniffed, opened the glove box, routed around inside, then asked, "Don't you have any damned tissues?"

That was more like it, more like the old Amanda. I reached over into the back, felt around on the floor, then handed her a box of Puffs.

"Take care. I'll be back."

I closed the car door, listened for the lock, then, satisfied, somewhat, I walked back onto the Channel 7 lot. Mike Willis and Joanne Snyder and a full team of forensic techs had arrived on the scene only minutes before and were already at work. Snyder, the head of CPD's ballistics department, had inserted a long, stiff rod through the two bullet holes and was sighting the line of fire. *Hell,* I thought, as I approached, *why bother. It's obvious.* I turned and looked at the two-story building on the opposite side of the road. Even from there, I could see the partially open window, second from the left on the top floor. I could also see there was something taped to the inside of the glass.

"Kate," I nodded in the direction of the building. "Second floor, second from the left. See it?"

She did. She grabbed Willis's arm, turned him around and pointed, "Let's get some people over there, Mike."

Mike Willis runs the CSI department at the Chattanooga PD. He nodded, tapped several of his techs, gave instructions, and the four of them loaded themselves into their van and headed out across the road, leaving Joanne Snyder alone to complete her search and assessment.

"We'd better get on over there, too," Kate said, as she nodded at Lonnie, "There's not a whole hell of a lot we can do here until the techs finish up. How's Amanda?"

"Not so good," I said, as the three of us walked together out of the Channel 7 lot and onto the sidewalk. "She's pretty shaken up, but she'll get over it."

Kate nodded but didn't answer.

"I'd like to say it was a near thing," I said, as we crossed the road, "but we all know it wasn't. She never was the target. The shooter's intention was to scare the crap out of her, but not just her. I'm thinking this was done for my benefit—if you can call it that. This thing has 'pro' written all over it. That shot—what was it, a hundred yards? — was within a quarter inch of dead center of a three-inch target. Think about that. It's not a shot an amateur could have made, even on his best day... well, one of five, maybe, but still."

I was deep in thought. My head full of questions, questions I couldn't answer, not yet. Who? Why?

Willis had left the door to the building open. We ran up the stairs to the second floor, Kate leading, Lonnie following me. At the top of the stairs, we entered a long corridor with a series of doors on either side. The second door was already

26

open but secured by the inevitable yellow and black tape. Mike and his crew, swathed from head to toe in white Tyvek coveralls, masks, and latex gloves were already at work inside the vacant room; there was nothing inside, not a single stick of furniture.

Even from the open doorway, I could see that the folded piece of paper taped to the partially open window had my name written on it, but we had to wait while Willis's tech processed the paper and the window before they could remove it.

Finally, after what seemed more like an hour than the ten minutes it actually was, Willis gently removed it from the glass and, holding it gingerly between his latex gloved forefinger and thumb, carried it across the room.

"Gloves please," he said and waited while we grabbed them from the box someone had placed on the floor just outside the door.

"Don't touch the tape, and finger and thumb only," he said as he handed it to me.

I took it from him, noting my name on the outside; the handwriting was the same as on the note to Amanda.

Still holding it between finger and thumb, I gently shook it open. The five words written inside made my blood run cold:

"Next time I won't miss."

And my first thought was, *Won't miss who? Amanda? Me? Who?*

My second thought was… I didn't have one. My mind had gone blank. I shook my head and handed the note to Kate. She stared down at it, then up at me. I shrugged. She looked again at the five words, and I watched as her face hardened: her eyes narrowed, her brow furrowed, and her lips set in a grim, half-smile. Yeah, she was smiling, but with little humor. I'd seen that smile before, and it boded no one any good.

"Kate?" I said.

She looked up at me. The smile was gone, her face softened, but now there was that look of determination I knew so well, and I knew without being told that we, Amanda and me… we weren't alone.

She handed the paper to Lonnie. He glanced down at it, and then up again and, wordlessly, handed the paper back to Willis who looked first at it, then at me, "What the hell is this about, Harry?" he asked.

"Somebody's trying to make a point, send a message. Hell of a way to do it, but effective, wouldn't you say?"

Willis nodded, slipped the note into an evidence bag, labeled it and signed and dated it.

"So what's the plan, Harry?" Kate asked.

"Geez. How the hell would I know? I told you what I think. Someone's out to cause grief, for me… and anyone connected to me, and that means not just Amanda, but you and the rest of my family too, maybe even my crew. Whoever did this is a pro, which means they'll finish what they've started, or at least try to. This could get ugly, Kate, really ugly. We have to find this son of a bitch, and quickly before someone dies. I'm going to have to get Amanda out of reach." I thought about it, shook my head, "and possibly my father and Rose too. Amanda's not going to go for that, and neither is August. Christ, what a… what a mess."

"We have a casing," Willis said, holding it up between finger and thumb for us to see. "It's a 5.56 NATO round, I say possibly fired from a semi-automatic rifle, an AR-15 or some such. It's clean. No prints, and whoever it was wanted to be sure we'd find it. It was on the window sill. Bizarre!"

I looked again at Kate, and then at Lonnie, "See what I mean? He's sending us, that is me, a message. The intent is clear: it's terrorism, but personal. It's me he's after. This is a psychological attack with the intent to instill… fear."

"What makes you think it's a he?" Kate asked. "The handwriting, on both notes, looks feminine to me. It could be a woman."

I nodded, the thought had struck me too, but that was even more bizarre. I knew of no woman that had an ax to grind with me, at least not on that level, and certainly none that could shoot the way this one could.

"Kate, I need to get Amanda home, and I need some space to think. I'm betting that whoever did this will move quickly, and that means I don't have time to screw around..." I looked her in the eye and said, "Look, I know I don't have to ask, but are you with me on this?"

She shrugged, "Of course. The case has already been assigned to me. Lonnie too," she looked at him. He nodded and smiled.

I had to make sure.

"Lonnie?" I asked.

"You know it, Harry," and I did, and that was a miracle in itself. Time was, and not so long ago, either, that Lonnie would happily have locked me up and thrown away the key. *My how time changes everything.*

"Thank you," I slapped him on the arm; he grinned.

"We'll get him, Harry."

"Or her," I said. "Okay. This is what I think we need to do..."

***

Calaway Jones, dressed in hiking gear—shorts, T-shirt, thick socks, boots, and a backpack—

looked no different from any other nineteen-year-old girl as she sat on the low stone wall some seventy yards, or so, to the north of the Starke home on East Brow Road. Swinging her legs, cell phone by her ear as she drank from a bottle of water, she watched as they arrived, one by one. She knew them all, by sight and by profile. She'd studied their files.

No one noticed her, the kid with the little camera taking pictures of the landscape. It was to be expected up there on the mountain; the views were spectacular. And certainly, no one noticed the Beretta Px4 Storm subcompact semi-automatic 9mm pistol that lay on the wall beside her. No, she blended into the background, just like any other kid out for an early evening hike, but Jones was no innocent youngster. Far from the nineteen years she affected so well, she was in fact thirty-five... and deadly.

Now, supposedly responsible for more than a dozen high-profile international assassinations around the world, she's been hired to, "take care of Harry Starke," but there were conditions in the contract. A quick kill was not what her employer wanted. Starke must be made to suffer, psychologically and physically, before she finally could "put him away." She had a plan, and so far, all was going well. There was only one small detail about the contract that bothered her, and it bothered her... a lot: she didn't know who her employer was. Her only contact with him was through a weird member of the African American community called Shady Tree.

She had no problem carrying out her contract to the letter. These people meant nothing to her. They were the enemy, to be exterminated as need be, but neither did she have any animosity toward them; they were a means to an end, and in the end it was, after all, just business.

She didn't like to kill for killing's sake, but would happily kill them all, if she thought she needed to, but she didn't think she would, need to. She was a master of intimidation; she was also a master of disguise; and she loved her job, which is exactly how she thought of it, as a job, employment. And she was expensive. The down payment on this contract—half—$125,000 was already in her numbered Swiss account; the rest would be paid when the job was complete. And it had better be paid; if not, her employer would become her ex-employer, with emphasis on the "ex."

By seven o'clock that evening, the gates to the Starke home were closed; the visitors—she'd counted eight—were all inside the house and she had what she wanted; it was time to go.

She slipped the Nikon Coolpix S9700 into her pocket—its long 25-750mm zoom lens had provided her with close-ups of each visitor. The Beretta she palmed and then slid it into one of the pockets in the backpack. Then she slipped down off the wall and resumed her leisurely walk. Twenty minutes later she was in the parking lot by Point Park where her Mini Cooper was parked. From there it was just a short drive down the mountain to the La Quinta Inn on Browns Ferry Road where she was staying.

Jones had arrived in the U.S. via a somewhat circuitous route from Paris where she lived alone in an apartment in the upscale 7th arrondissement, just a short walk from the Champ de Mars where she loved to stroll, or just sit and watch the world go by. She'd traveled to the U.S. as Genevieve Charon, a twenty-two-year-old French student— she spoke the language fluently—on a genuine French passport—one of a half-dozen she still maintained from her time in the Mossad. The reason for her visit was to tour some of the Civil War battlefields, something she had absolutely no interest in, but was a reason good enough to acquire a visa without having to answer a lot of questions.

Purely out of habit, she checked the strand of hair on the outside of the hotel guest room door; it was still in place. She had no reason to think it wouldn't be, but still… She dumped her backpack on the sofa, checked her computer—it too was undisturbed—and then flopped down on the bed, turned her head to look at the time, smiled—it was a little after eight—sighed contentedly, and closed her eyes. It had been a good day, a good beginning.

33

She picked up her iPhone, dialed a number, listened intently, smiled as she recognized Harry Starke's voice, then she turned on the speaker and set it down on the nightstand. The conversation in the Starke home came through loud and clear. It wasn't many minutes later when the iPhone dinged—an alert. She picked it up, looked at the screen and smiled. *Harry's making a call.*

She sat up and, unbeknownst to Harry Starke, listened in on the call.

Chapter 4
Tuesday, July 11, 6pm

It had been one hell of a day, and it wasn't yet over, but now we were at home on the mountain. Amanda was feeling better, but I wasn't. She'd soon realized that the shot was not meant to do her harm, and over the past several hours the shock of what had happened had worn off. Now she was busily preparing to receive our guests. Me? I was already halfway into my second double shot of Laphroaig, and it was not yet six o'clock.

I was in the small room I called my office, seated on the sofa in front of the picture window, staring out at the amazing view of the city and the river. I looked at it, but I didn't *see* it if you know what I mean. If you've ever driven the interstate, lost in thought, and then wondered how the hell you managed to survive that last three miles, you know exactly what I mean. That's how it was that early evening.

Talk about visions—I couldn't clear my head of them. I had flashbacks, I had fantasies, bad fantasies, images of death… most of it at my own hands. I was suffering a waking nightmare, until… I realized I was playing right into the shooter's plan. This was exactly what he, or she, wanted. *Shit! Psychological warfare. Hmmm. Two can play at that game. I wonder… Yes. Oh yeah.*

Harper! Tomorrow… I couldn't help but smile at the thought.

I looked at my watch. It was time for the early evening news. I picked up the remote, turned on the TV, flipped the channels to 7, and settled down to watch. Charlie had the lead story; I hit the record button.

"Earlier today," Pitbull Charlie said, he was outside with his back to the main entrance of the Channel 7 building, "there was a bizarre shooting incident right here at Channel 7, in our own parking lot. The target, so it seems, was one of our anchors, Amanda Cole, wife of private investigator Harry Starke, but was she the target?" he asked, dramatically.

The live image was replaced by an earlier image of Amanda and me surrounded by police officers. That lasted maybe five seconds before switching back to Charlie. "It appears that the shot was not intended to kill, or even wound Amanda, but to frighten her, to strike terror deep into her heart, and that it certainly did." *Oh geez, they do love to lay it on.*

"The police are not releasing much information, and neither are Starke or Amanda, but what we do know is that a shot fired from some sort of sniper rifle hit Amanda's SUV narrowly missing her head. I say the shot was not intended for Amanda because it was obviously taken by an expert sniper who could easily have killed her had he wanted to.

36

I can tell you that with some confidence because a small target—actually, it was a smiley face—about three inches in diameter was stuck to the driver's side window of her car and..." he paused for effect, "the bullet, fired from the second-floor window of a building more than one hundred yards away across the street, hit the target less than a quarter inch from dead center. Amanda also found a note under her windshield wiper. What it said, we don't know. Amanda is not saying, and the police aren't releasing the details, at least not yet. For Channel 7 News, this is Charlie Grove."

Parts of the same story also ran on the national ABC and Fox News networks on the six-thirty news, and by then our guests were beginning to arrive. Bob Ryan, my lead investigator, and Kate Gazzara came together—they'd been an item for almost a year now. Jacque arrived some ten minutes later, then my father and stepmother followed by Tim Clarke, my personal computer geek. Sergeant Lonnie Guest was next and finally Ronnie Hall, my white collar crime investigator. Heather Stillwell, my number two investigator after Bob, was on a cruise in the Caribbean.

I had them assemble in the living room. They'd all been to the house before, so the stunning view from the picture window was no distraction. The mood was somber, quiet. Amanda had made sandwiches. They were served buffet-style along with iced tea or lemonade; an assortment of stronger stuff was also available for those that wanted it. Only me, Amanda and August did.

I seated myself on the arm of the sofa next to Amanda, set my drink down on the coffee table, picked up my iPad and stylus, flipped open Notes, and looked around the group. They all stared back at me; I had their attention.

"Thank you all for coming," I began. "I wish… well, I wish it was under different circumstances. You all know what happened at Channel 7 this morning. What the hell it was about, I still have no idea…" I paused, stared down at the iPad, then continued. "No, I don't know, but I have a feeling it's just the beginning, the opening shot—literally. Someone has an agenda. I've thought about it, and I figure it has to be someone I've hurt in the past. Three names come to mind, Salvatore DeLuca's younger brother, Tony, Vincent Sirocco, and Gordon Harper, Little Billy. Thoughts, anyone?"

"DeLuca, maybe," Bob said. "Sirocco? I don't think so. That was almost six years ago…"

"Yeah," Lonnie interrupted him, "and six years is plenty of time for him to stew and fester. He would be my pick, after Harper."

Bob nodded. So did Kate, and Jacque.

"Anyone else?" I asked.

"Harper," Kate said. "Bob killed Sal DeLuca, so Tony's running the restaurant now, and he seems happy enough. He's a different animal; not at all like Sal. Sirocco? Could be, I suppose, but I like Harper for it. He's a vicious son of a bitch, and he threatened you, remember? And more than once, as I recall."

I did, and she was right. Not only had I put him away for what was probably the rest of his life, but I'd also killed his daughter and her husband.

"Harper, then. I agree," I said, "but we should keep an open mind. It could be one of the others, or even someone else. I've made a lot of enemies over the years."

Kate nodded, "We, Lonnie and me, officially have the case and, if need be, we can take some leave—we both have plenty owing. What's the plan, Harry? Do you have one?"

I started to shake my head, then, "Well, the first thing we need do is get everyone out of danger, and that's almost everyone here."

I looked at Rose, then at August; he was slowly shaking his head. Amanda put her hand on my knee, squeezed hard and looked up at me, also shaking her head. The rest of them sat still, silent.

"Bob, I know. There's no way you're going anywhere."

He grinned, "You got that right!"

"Jacque, Tim, Ronnie…" I had to smile; they were all shaking their heads. "Sorry, guys. It's not up for discussion. You're fired, all of you. I have checks for each of you…"

"What? What d'hell you tinkin'? Ain' happnin',
It… Ain't… Gonna… Happen. You hear?" The
Jamaican accent was as strong as I'd ever heard it,
and I believed her. Jacque had her ass in her
hands, and she wasn't about to take no for an
answer, but I'd known how she would react, and
all I could do was shake my head.

"What she said," Ronnie said, quietly. "That
goes for me too."

"And for me," Tim said.

I heaved a sigh, then nodded. It was what I'd
expected, and I knew there was no point in
arguing.

"Okay, if that's the way you want it…" I
looked at each of them in turn, then said, "Thanks,
guys. I love you too… Ronnie," I looked hard at
him, "are you sure? You played a big part in
putting Harper away. You testified against him. If
it is him…"

He shrugged, "I'm not going anywhere, Harry."

"Okay. It's your call."

I looked at August, then at Rose. August
opened his mouth to speak, but I held up my hand
to stop him.

"Forget it, Dad. You're almost seventy years
old…" I thought he was going to jump out of his
chair. "And you have to think of Rose…"

"Bullshit!" Rose said, angrily.

"Look. This bastard is out to hurt me, and probably kill me too. He can do that, hurt me, by hurting… or killing, the people I love. That makes me vulnerable. Rose; you, Dad, and Amanda have to leave, get far away from here. Dad, I want you to call Joe and have him ready the Gulfstream, and then I want the three of you to go straight from here to Lovell Field and get the hell out of the country. Yeah, I know, passports and luggage. Forget 'em. You go first to Puerto Rico; you shop there, and I'll FedEx the passports to you; from there you can go where you like. No, Dad, I don't want to hear it."

"Well, you're going to. I can't just up and leave. Who the hell do you think will handle my cases?"

"Christ, Dad. You have dozens of associate attorneys working for you. Pick one, or two, for God's sake. You're going."

He looked at me as if he'd been snake-bit but, reluctantly, he nodded. The me being vulnerable thing he understood.

Amanda rose to her feet and walked to the door, "It's not happening, Harry. I won't go; you can't make me." And she slammed the door behind her.

"Oh for Christ's sake," I groaned. I shook my head. *I'll deal with her later,* I thought, knowing damn well I wouldn't.

"You want me to go with her?" Bob asked.

"No. She'll be fine. Dad, make the call, now."
And he did.

"Bob. I'd like for you to take them to the airport okay?"

"No problem. You want me to take them now?"

"Yeah, well, in a few minutes. First, we need to talk about what we're going to do next."

"And what would that be?" Jacque asked, the Jamaican accent gone with her anger.

"Well, the first thing we have to do is try to flush him out."

"And how do you plan to do that?" Kate asked.

"We use the media, Channel 7; Pitbull Charlie—no, Amanda's not going anywhere near that place. The best form of defense is attack, right?"

"If you know who the hell to attack," Lonnie said. "We don't."

"Not yet, we don't. But we know that whoever it is, is a pro, right? Pro's don't make mistakes. So we put it out there that she did, make a mistake.

"From the handwriting on the notes, we think it might be a woman, but we don't know for sure; maybe it is, and maybe it isn't; it doesn't matter. But if it is a woman, and we release that to the public, on air, what kind of an effect do you think it will have on her? It might shake her up a bit. At the very least, it will give her something to think about. She'll wonder how the hell we've gotten

42

onto her so soon. If we're wrong and it's a guy, well, no harm done. He'll feel like a winner. Thoughts, anyone?"

"I don't like it, Harry," Kate said. "Oh, not the story thing; I just don't like all of us walking around blind, you in particular. You're a hell of a big target, and she, if it is a she, doesn't miss. She's already proved that."

"True, but it is what it is. I'll wear a vest from now on, whenever I'm out of the house. So will the rest of you." *Vest? Not worth a damn against a head shot, or a 5.56 for that matter, not unless it hits the plates, but better than nothing.*

"And, from now on, you all go armed. Jacque?"

She nodded, reached behind her, and brought forth the M&P9 I'd given her.

"Tim? Ronnie?"

"Mine's in the glove box," Tim said.

"Mine, too," Ronnie looked at me sheepishly.

"They'll do no good there. From now, you carry, right?" They both nodded.

I looked at Bob. He grinned at me, then opened his lightweight golf jacket to reveal the twin .45 compact Sig 1911s hanging under his arms.

"Hah!" I said.

I didn't bother to ask Kate and Lonnie. I knew they were always armed.

"Okay," I said, "just a couple more things, and then you can get out of here. The consensus seems to be that Harper is behind it. If so, I guarantee that Shady is involved... No. I know; he's not the shooter. He's not good enough, nor does he have the balls for it, but he probably knows who is." I thought for a minute, then looked at my watch. It was just after nine o'clock and still light outside.

"Kate, Lonnie. When we're done here, how about we visit the Sorbonne? If anyone knows where we can find Shady, we'll find them there."

They nodded.

"Good. First though, I need to call Charlie Grove, give him something to run with on the eleven o'clock news. Tomorrow, I'll drive to Atlanta and see Harper. He's not going to admit anything, but if it is him, he'll let me know—he can't help himself—and then at least we'll know for sure, and maybe we'll be able to figure out some sort of a plan.

"Dad. Have Joe call me as soon as you get to the airport. In the meantime, figure out where you two are going after Puerto Rico. No, I don't want to know, and you're to tell no one. You call me four times a day—no more than five seconds a call—at eight in the morning, noon, five o'clock, and ten. If you miss a call by more than thirty minutes, I'll know something is wrong, and I'll get ahold of Joe and come after you. All clear?"

He nodded.

"Bob, take them to the airport, please, and then come back here and stay with Amanda while we go to the Sorbonne. We won't leave until you return, okay?"

"Got it. Anything else?"

"No. Not for now, anyway. I'll deal with Amanda later, or not."

He grinned, "Not, I should think."

I hugged August and Rose, said my goodbyes, and then watched as Bob hustled them out. August looked pale, frail. He was beginning to show his age, bless him. Rose? Well, Rose is Rose.

I gave instructions to Jacque, Tim and Ronnie to go straight from our meeting to the office and fit themselves out with vests—I had a half-dozen Point Blank Spider Tactical vests with ceramic plates in the storeroom. I also kept two more at the house: one for me and one for Amanda. No, I couldn't wear the plates all the time, they're too damned heavy and inconvenient. Amanda, though: I'd make sure she wore them.

Me? Paranoid? You betcha.

And so I turned them all loose—all except Kate and Lonnie—telling them if I caught them not wearing the vests, including the plates, I really would fire them. *Yeah, and they believed me, not.*

***

Harper's face was a mask as he ran the recording of the early evening news on his iPad for the umpteenth time, but inside... he was smiling, delighted at the beginning. *My, my, Harry,* he thought. *The lady does look upset. Your turn soon, you piece of shit!*

***

Calaway Jones looked at her watch and set her alarm an hour ahead for nine o'clock that evening. Then she smiled, laced her fingers together behind her neck, lay back on the pillows, and closed her eyes. She was still smiling when she fell asleep. She'd heard every word; everything Harry Starke and his crew knew, she knew too. *So,* she thought as she drifted off, *Billy Harper's the one who hired me. I must talk to Shady about that...* And she drifted off into a deep, dreamless sleep,

She woke an hour later to the buzzing of the alarm. She showered, dressed, and feeling refreshed and ready for whatever the evening might bring, she headed for the door.

Chapter 5
Tuesday, July 11, 9pm

After talking strategy for a while, I left Kate and Lonnie in the living room and went to find Amanda. I found her out on the patio, seated on the low stone wall that separated the pool area from the gardens. She sat with her hands on the wall on either side of her, staring down on the city spread out like a jeweled carpet below. It was still light, but the lights were already on in Chattanooga.

I sat down beside her, slipped my arm around her waist, and pulled her toward me; she resisted, tried to pull away, said nothing.

"Amanda, we need to talk."

"So talk."

"I want you out of here. I don't want you to get hurt."

No answer.

I sighed, "Honey, whoever is doing this, is very, very good, and deadly serious…"

"Don't talk to me like I'm a baby; I'm not." She turned toward me; her face only inches from mine. I could feel her breath on my lips.

"Harry, I'm not going anywhere. I'm not leaving you here to face this alone."

"I won't be alone. I have Kate and Bob and Lonnie…"

"Hah!" She turned away.

"What do you mean, hah?"

She didn't answer.

"Look. At least think about it…"

"There's nothing to think about."

I sighed, shook my head, squeezed her waist, leaned in and nibbled on her ear.

"And you can quit that. It won't work. Not this time."

"Okay, you win. Bob's taken August and Rose to the airport," I looked at my watch. "He shouldn't be long. I'll wait with you until he returns and then he'll stay with you while we run down to the Sorbonne. I want to talk to…"

"Oh no, you don't. You're not going anywhere without me."

"Amanda…"

"Forget it, Harry. It's not happening."

I shook my head, exasperated, then said, "Geez, the fat little bastard will think he's being raided."

"Do him good; fat little…" She didn't finish the thought, and I knew she didn't mean it anyway. Yes, Benny Hinkle is a fat little bastard, but he has a good heart, and he thinks the world of Amanda, and she knows it.

The little creep is almost as wide as he is tall, almost always unshaven, one of Chattanooga's undead, a creature of the night that creeps about his lair, the Sorbonne, coming out only at night to short his customers on watered liquor and deafen them with mind-numbing noise from a jukebox that's older than he is... Ah, maybe I'm being too hard on the little guy.

The Sorbonne is Chattanooga's last refuge for the city's night crawlers, a sleazy downtown bar— Benny calls it a night club. I knew the place well, and Benny even better. Even now that I was married, I spent more time in there than I probably should—it could be fun, in a warped sort of way— but mostly I went there to gather information, and to keep an eye on the lowlifes that inhabit the place. That night was no different. I wanted information, and I wanted it quick, and I figured Bennie could supply it. If not, he would know who could.

I heard the electronic gate open. I looked at my watch. It was almost nine o'clock.

"Okay," I said, taking her hand, "I hear Bob's car. I'll have a quick word with him, and I need to make a call, and then we'll go. I left my phone in the kitchen. It's still early...ish, and I want to beat the rush and the noise."

"I'll need to change first," she said, stepping down off the wall.

I shook my head. She was wearing skinny jeans and a white T-shirt.

"No you don't. You looked great."

"Sez you. I'll be just a minute."

We entered the house, and she went to the bedroom.

Bob was in the living room talking to Kate.

"Hey," I said. "You get them away okay?"

"Yep. I watched them take off. August called Leo from the car. He'll have his chopper waiting for them when they land. So they're fine."

I nodded. Leo Martan, a long-time family friend, owned an estate on Calypso Key east of Puerto Rico. Earlier in the year, Kate and I had solved his daughter's murder. It was a good choice; Leo would look after them.

When Amanda emerged five minutes later, she was wearing one of those little black dresses that women seem so fond of... and I have to admit I was kind of partial to them myself. A pair of red three-inch heels and a red leather clutch completed the picture. She looked stunning, and that was really not appropriate for where we were going. Be that as it may, I kissed her, told her she looked lovely and, along with Kate, Bob, and Lonnie, we headed out to the cars. Kate would ride with Bob, and I would follow them; Lonnie would follow me.

I held open the door of the Maxima for Amanda, then walked around to the driver's side and dropped heavily into the seat. As I did so, she let out a screech that made me think I'd hurt her in some way, but then I saw what it was.

Oh shit! I stared at the round, yellow smiley face sticker in the center of the windshield staring in at me. My guts turned to liquid. *When? How did they get past the alarm? Geez! It must have been turned off. Son of a bitch…*

"It's okay," I said, taking her hand and squeezing it. "It's just a sticker. I'll get it."

I jumped out, pulled it off, trying not to touch its surface. Then I got back into the car and carefully placed it on the back seat.

I looked at Amanda. Her face was set, and she was staring straight forward out through the windshield. Even in the rapidly lowering light, I could see her face had lost its color.

I took her hand again and said, gently, "It's okay. It's nothing. Just a practical joke, is all."

"Like the one at Channel 7 this morning?" she asked, without looking at me.

There was nothing I could say. I thumbed the starter, put the car in drive, and rolled onto East Brow; the electronic gates closing slowly behind me.

Damn! What next…? I thought as I made the turn onto Scenic Highway. *This car has got to go, and before I go to Atlanta tomorrow. I bet the damn thing is bugged. I need to call Lennie. I'll do it first thing in the morning. We'll have to get rid of the Lexus, too.*

Chapter 6
Tuesday, July 11, 10:30pm

We parked on Market and walked the two blocks to the Sorbonne. The side street—hell it was more alleyway than it was a street—was dark, lit only by a single sodium lamp that turned the walls and walkway a haunting orange color. The sign over the door was lit, but several of the bulbs were shot; instead of Sorbonne it read only, "bon e." The entrance, a small square porch with windows on either side, was a black hole that stank of stale urine.

"Listen," I said to Amanda, "Let's keep the sticker thing to ourselves, at least for now. Okay?"

"Whatever you say, Harry."

Inside the Sorbonne, the lights were dim, the music a cacophony of rap at one end of the bar and a TV blaring out news from CNN at the other. The place was almost empty—it was, after all, a Tuesday night. Laura was leaning on the bar flashing her more than ample assets at a semi-drunk youngster that looked to be barely old enough to be allowed inside the place. Laura was working for tips.

Laura Davies was Benny's partner. She'd been an institution at the Sorbonne for as long as I could remember. The two were as incongruous a pair as you could imagine. What their arrangement was,

I'd never been able to figure, romantic or monetary. I hoped it wasn't the former; the picture painted by the idea made me shudder.

She's quite a character, is Laura: Daisy Duke on steroids, a tall, slightly overweight blonde, usually attired in a tank top that barely covers her... yeah, I have to admit it, magnificent breasts. Add a pair of cutoff jeans that barely cover her ass, and cowboy boots, and, well, you get the picture. At first impression, you'd think she was a whore; she isn't. She is, in fact, a peach, and I like her, a lot. Peach she might be, but she is no pushover: she, in the words of the song, "ruled her smoky kingdom" with an iron fist—a sawed off baseball bat she kept handy under the bar.

"Hey, Harry, Amanda. How the hell are you?" She left the source of her income with his elbows in a pool of beer, his head cocked awkwardly to one side, and a bleary look on his face, trying to figure out where she'd gone.

"Ahhh shit!" Benny growled as he flung the filthy washcloth down into the sink behind the bar. "An' I was lookin' forward to a quiet night. How many times, Harry, do I have to ask you to stay the hell out of my club? Hey, nice to see you, Mrs. Starke. Oooh, the sound o' that leaves a nasty taste in m' mouth. How come you had to go an' marry the mutt? Hell, you always had him right where you wanted him. You all right, by the way? I saw that thing on TV. You got shot at."

"Nice to see you too, Benny," I growled sarcastically.

"Hello, Benny," Amanda said, as she leaned across the bar and kissed his cheek. "Yes, I'm fine. It's good to see you too."

He grinned wickedly at her, winked at me, picked up the nasty cloth and proceeded to wipe out a somewhat crusty-looking glass with it; inwardly I shuddered.

"Hey Kate, Lonnie… Bob," he said, waving the cloth at them. "Geez, Harry, you bringing cops in here will give the place a bad name. What'll you have folks? Amanda?"

"Gin and tonic please, Benny, and in a plastic cup, if you don't mind."

"Yeah, and make sure it's a new one," I said.

He looked wounded but complied. He pulled a white half-pint cup out of a sleeve at the back of the bar, scooped ice into it, splashed what looked like a quad measure of Bombay Sapphire into it, then topped it off with a thimbleful of tonic. Any more than one of those and I'd be carrying her out.

"I'll have the same," I said, as Laura looked after the needs of the others. And I did, only somehow it wasn't quite the same. The little bastard had reversed the measure; mine was just about all tonic and ice. I looked at him, he grinned, shrugged, and was about to turn away when I asked him if we could talk.

55

"You got a minute, Benny? We need to talk."

"Yeah, I figured as much. You never come in here these days without wanting something. Gi' me a minute an' I'll be with you. Why don't you grab that table over there, in the corner?" And we did.

"So," he said, dropping his oversized rear onto a chair that rocked dangerously as it took the weight. "What do you want. Is it something to do with what happened to Amanda?"

"It is. What's the word on the street?"

"How the hell would I know? I never get out on the street."

"You know what I mean."

He nodded, looked serious, then said, "I had a couple of friends of yours in here on—hmmm, when was it?—A couple of weeks ago, on a Friday, I think: Shady and Duvon. Shady asked if I'd seen you. I told him no, which was the truth."

"And you didn't think to call me?"

He shrugged, "Didn't seem too important. He said it in passing, like it was an afterthought, although…"

"What else did he say?" Kate asked.

"Just conversation. Said he'd heard you'd gotten married, Harry, to Amanda. I didn't think nothin' of it; you two have a history, so I figured he was just curious, why? Is it important? Now I think of it, he asked about you too, Kate. Wanted to know if you ever came in here. He was lookin' around when he asked. I figured he was worried about maybe runnin' into you, the cop thing, right?"

Kate looked at me, her eyebrows arched in question. I shook my head, and said, "Think about it, Benny. Was he just shooting the bull, or did he have an agenda?"

"Just shootin' the bull, I think, but who knows? He's a devious bastard; you know that, Harry. I was surprised to see him, though. Was a time when he was in here almost every night, then I didn't see him for six or more months, until that Friday, an' he ain't been back since... so... Hell, on thinkin' about it, maybe he was diggin' for info... Oh shit! Was it him? Was him what shot at you, Amanda."

She didn't answer; I did, "No. Not him, at least I don't think so, but I sure as hell will find out. Where's he living, hanging out? Do you know?"

He shook his head, "Harry, I thought he was long gone. It was a surprise to see him after all that time."

"Well," I said. "I need you to find out, and quickly. Yeah?"

He nodded, thoughtfully, then said, "I'll do my best. Might take a day or two, dependin' on how bad he wants to stay hid. Gi'me a couple-a- days an' if I find anything, I'll call you... Wait a minute. Maybe Laura knows something." He turned in his chair and called her over.

"Talk to Harry, Laura," he said when she arrived. "I'll take the bar 'til you're done."

He left, and Laura slid her stunning backside onto the chair. "Umm. Still warm," she said. I couldn't help but shudder at the picture that presented.

"Oh come on, Harry. I'm just funning with you. What do you need?"

"Benny tells me Shady and his running back, Duvon James, were in a couple of weeks ago. You know what they were after?"

"Apart from a couple of seedy-looking hookers that were camped out at the far end of the bar, no, I don't. Is it important?"

"Could be. Do you know where he's hanging out?"

"No, I seen him a couple of times at the Mellow and once in the Grill, other than that…"

She was talking about the Mellow Mushroom and the Big River Grill.

"Well," I said. "I need to find him, talk to him. If you hear anything, give me a call will you, please?"

"You know it, Harry. I'll pin my ears back, 'kay?"

I nodded, thanked her, and she got up and left, returned to her spot behind the bar and once more offered her mark a view of a landscape the poor sucker would likely never forget.

"So. What do you think?" Bob asked. "It's too much of a coincidence that he was in here asking after you, right?"

"Yeah, I think so," I said. "It has Harper's mark all over it."

"Oh my God, Harry," Amanda said, squeezing my arm, "please don't say that."

"It has to be," I said. "Benny's right. Shady disappeared that night up in Cleveland. I thought he was gone for good but, now it seems he's back, and that can't be for any good reason."

"He's working for Harper," Kate said. "You know it; I know it, but I just don't see either one of them on the back end of a sniper rifle. That was one hell of a shot for an AR if that's what it was, even with a scope. They're not that good, either of 'em."

I nodded, she was right.

"If what you say is true," Amanda said, "if it is Harper, maybe he used Shady as the procurer. If there is a contract, someone would have to do the hiring. He couldn't do that from inside the prison, could he?"

"Money talks, Amanda," I said, thoughtfully. "There's no telling who he has in his pocket, inside the tank and out. But you're right. Shady may be the key. We have to find him, talk to him.

In the meantime, I'll go to Atlanta and talk to Harper and find out if it is him. Maybe then I can figure out what to do about it. One thing's for sure, whoever it is he's hired is a pro, and one cocky bastard too."

I looked around the table. The mood, to say the least, was somber.

"Let's get out of here," I said. "One drink of water is enough for me. I need something stronger." And we did.

***

Nobody noticed the black Mini Cooper parked in the shadows fifty yards away down the street.

It was after one in the morning when Calaway returned to her room. She showered, slipped into a jade green set of Olivia Von Halle silk pajamas, plumped up the pillows and, with her laptop on her knees, settled comfortably back against the headboard.

For once, it hadn't all gone her way. The conversation in the bar had been drowned out by the noise: the music and the TV. *Oh well,* she thought. *You can't win 'em all.*

She opened the computer and went straight to the Channel 7 website and ran the eleven o'clock newscast, and she smiled.

You have to be kidding me, she thought, as she watched Charlie Grove's segment.

"We have an update on the shooting that occurred right here at Channel 7 earlier this evening. A confidential source within the Chattanooga police department has revealed that they are looking for a woman. They believe she is probably aged between thirty and forty and masquerading as a tourist…"

She closed the laptop, put it to one side on the bed, then leaned back against the headboard and closed her eyes.

Nice try, Harry, but it won't work; you know nothing. Wish I could've heard what went on in the bar… Hmmm.

Thirty seconds later she was asleep, a deep, dreamless sleep.

Chapter 7
Wednesday, July 12, Noon
USP Atlanta

I didn't sleep a whole lot that night either and, for once, neither did Amanda. She was in a mood for something more than sleep and I, I have to admit, was only too pleased to supply it. It was well after midnight when we got home but, late as it was, we decided to go for a swim. I locked the gates, set the alarm and checked the monitors: nothing, but I wasn't taking any chances. I set my VP9 poolside, on the apron, handy enough, should I need it.

The water was a comfortable eighty degrees, and we swam together naked for fifteen or twenty minutes, and then we made love under the stars, gently, on one of the loungers. And then we went inside and did it again, only with a little more passion. It must have been almost three in the morning when I finally dropped off to sleep.

I woke early the next day... well, it was almost six—less than three hours of shut-eye; I'd regret it later, no doubt, so I decided to forgo my usual two-mile run, but not because I was tired, but for a couple of other reasons. One, I had a lot on my mind and two, I didn't know what I might run into. That sticker on my windshield didn't get there by itself. So I made coffee for two, sat down on the side of the bed, Amanda's side, and looked down at her. She had one eye half open and was smiling up at me; all thoughts of what had happened yesterday apparently gone, or so I hoped.

"Do you think we did it?" she asked.

"Did what?" I was puzzled.

"Got pregnant, of course."

"What?"

"I'm ovulating. It could happen. I hope it did."

"Amanda, we talked about that, but we didn't decide… anything."

"You didn't," she said, mischievously.

"We'll talk about it again, later, when I've gotten through this mess. Until then…"

"It's not going to change anything," she said, rolling over onto her back, arms and legs stretched wide. "You want to try again?" The smile on her face was one that was hard to resist, but I did.

"Yeah, I want to try again, but I'm not going to. Now get your lazy rear out of bed. I have things I need to do before I leave…"

"Ooh, goody,"

I looked at her. She kicked off the sheets. She was wearing nothing but her skin and still smiling innocently up at me, "No, Amanda, you're not one of them." *Sometimes my willpower amazes even me.*

We had a quiet breakfast together and then I called Bob, then Kate, then Jacque, got them all squared away and then I had another thought: *visiting hours at USP?*

I went to my office, fired up my iMac, and pulled up the prison website, *Damn it! General visiting hours: Friday, Saturday, Sunday and Holidays. Today is Wednesday. Damn, Damn, Damn. Wait, I have an idea.*

It was early, but what the hell; I had no choice. I called my weekend golfing partner, Federal Judge Henry Strange and told him what I needed. He told me he'd make a couple of calls and get back to me, and he did. Three minutes later, he called me back: I had an appointment at noon. *Good, no great. Now I need to get rid of the Maxima. That thing has become a liability.*

I called my buddy, Lennie Brewster, at Mountain View Chevrolet.

"Hey, Lennie. I'm in a bind. I need a car, and I need it fast, something quick… but not a Corvette. What do you have?"

"Oh boy, did you ever call at just the right time? Come on *down.* I have something a little bit special to show you."

"What is it? Is it ready to roll? I need in and out and gone as quick as possible."

"It's a Camaro ZL1 automatic, ten speed. Ready to go? Well, I'll need to fill the tank and run it through the wash…"

"Don't bother with the wash, Lennie. I don't have time. Just fill it up. How much is it? I'll have a check for you. You can give me what you can for the Maxima whenever you have time to figure it out."

"Harry! You need to test drive it. This sucker is a beast. Zero to sixty in three-point-five seconds. You just don't just do this without a trial, and I'll need to show you how everything works."

"Lennie, it's a car, for Christ's sake. I can figure all that out for myself. I'll be there in thirty minutes, maybe a little more. How much?"

"Geez, Harry. Sixty-two, less the trade-in, plus tax. It should be sixty-four-five, but I'll cut you a deal. I'll have the paperwork ready by the time you get here, but I won't be able to figure what you owe until I know what I can give you for the Nissan."

"Good enough, Lennie. Gotta go."

I returned to the kitchen where Amanda was sitting at the breakfast bar. She was wearing one of my T-shirts and boxer pajama bottoms. Her hair was a mess, but she still looked stunning. She had her feet up on the footrest of the bar stool, her elbows on the bar top, and was cradling a huge mug of steaming coffee to her lips. She raised her eyebrows as I sat down.

65

"When are you leaving?" she asked, through the steam.

"As soon as Bob gets here. He'll stay with you until I get back."

"Atlanta, huh?"

"Yup, but first I'm trading in the Maxima. It's too well known. I have an appointment with Lennie at Mountain View. He has something for me. We'll get rid of the Lexus too, as soon as they release it."

She set the mug down on the bar top and leaned back against the rest. "Harry, I love my Lexus," she said, quietly.

"We'll get you another... when this is all over..."

She looked up at me through her lashes, I thought she was going to say it—"If we survive"—but she didn't. Instead, she nodded and picked up her cup.

There was a beep from the monitor. I looked up at it and saw that Bob was outside the gate.

"It's Bob. Go get dressed. I'll let him in." She did, and I went to the panel and thumbed the buttons to turn off the alarm and open the gate.

"Coffee?" I asked as he ambled into the kitchen and dropped heavily onto the stool Amanda had just vacated.

"Oh yeah, but decaf. I'm wired. Where's Amanda? She okay?"

I nodded, "Getting dressed. She'll be but a minute. Listen: Don't let her out of your sight today. Don't let her leave the house unless you absolutely have to; if you do, you go with her. Don't turn off the alarms. Don't open the gates… and for God's sake make sure she wears her vest."

"Geez, Harry, whadda you think I am? I been doing this shit for more years than you. I know what I'm doin'. Okay?"

"Yeah. So you do. Sorry."

Amanda returned, and I made ready to leave. I didn't want to because it was then I had one of those god-awful feelings of impending doom. I took a deep breath, looked at Bob, eyebrows raised. He smiled, nodded, and said, "Go on. Get out of here, Harry. Amanda and me, we got things to do, don't we, girl?"

She smiled at him, fondly.

I shrugged, shook my head once, grabbed her by the shoulders, kissed her on the lips, perhaps a little longer than I should have and then, reluctantly, I took my leave.

Fifteen minutes later, I swung the Maxima onto the dealership lot; Lennie was outside, waiting for me. He was standing beside a metallic gray—Nighthawk Gray, I learned later—Camaro, a car I was somewhat familiar with, the older models, that is, although I'd never driven one. But this one… well, it was unlike anything I'd ever seen, let alone driven, before.

"Here, Lennie," I said, sliding out of the Maxima and tossing the keys to him. "See what you can give me for this one. No, not now. I'll drop by tomorrow, well sometime."

"You got it. Whaddaya think, Harry?" He gazed proudly at the shiny gray monster. "Six hundred and fifty horses; six point two liter V-8; ten-speed automatic, supercharger, zero to sixty before you can count to four, 180 miles an hour. It cooks, Harry, it cooks!"

"Looks good, Lennie, but I gotta go. In the meantime, here's the check. You fill in the number. I trust you. Where do I sign?"

"Damn it, Harry. For God's sake slow down and take a breath…"

"Lennie. I told you; I don't have time for this. Now is it ready or do I need to do what I have to in the Maxima?"

He sighed, "Okay, come on inside. It'll take but a minute. I have the papers already filled out. There's a temporary tag in the rear windshield, and the tank's full."

Less than five minutes later, he handed me the keys, if you could call them that, two sets—the car had keyless ignition.

"Harry, for Christ's sake be careful," he said, worriedly. "Go real steady on the gas until you're used to it…"

"Yeah, Lennie. I'll figure it out. I gotta go. I have an appointment in Atlanta at noon, okay?"

He looked at his watch, "You'll make it with time to spare, depending on how many tickets you get." He grinned at me.

I got in, closed the door, buckled up and looked around—*Er, I see what you mean,* I thought. *It's like a damned jet fighter.* I found the starter, put my foot on the brake pedal and pushed the button. The big V-8 caught immediately and rumbled softly, waiting. I had the feeling I was about to be launched into space. I flipped the gas pedal gently; I felt the torque as the damn thing roared like a wounded lion. *Wow!*

I looked out of the side window at Lennie. He had his hands in his pockets, grinning at me and shaking his head.

I nodded at him, smiled, took a deep breath, shifted into drive—a damned button on the center console—touched the gas pedal, let off the parking brake, and the car rumbled slowly forward and out onto 20th Street heading toward Market. Lennie hadn't been exaggerating; the car was a damned beast all right, but oh boy was it smooth.

I twitched the gas pedal; the car leaped forward. It was only by sheer instinct that I managed to avoid running into the rear end of a flatbed truck that was waiting for the light.

The light changed. I took another deep breath, eased the car left onto Market, then right onto the southbound ramp and up onto I-24, and then I felt a little better, but not much. I cruised on up through the Ridge Cut at close to seventy miles an hour, my foot barely touching the gas pedal. A minute or so later, I was through the Split, over the Georgia State Line, heading southeast toward Atlanta, and it was only then that I was able to relax, a little. The big engine was purring like a happy panther, and I settled back and let the leather enfold me, and then I took a minute to glance around the interior of my new pet; the damned thing even had a HUD, a heads-up display. *How cool is that? Geez, this is the life. Why didn't I get one of these babies sooner?*

I set the cruise control to seventy-seven—no point in getting a ticket—and settled down to enjoy the ride. Every once in a while, to overtake a slower vehicle, or just for the hell of it, I'd drop her out of cruise, slip the gear shift to manual, and hit the gas and flip the paddle through the gears. The response was… instantaneous and brutal. I was going to love this car. By the time I hit I-285 east of Marietta, I'd gotten used to the beast, well… somewhat, and was feeling like a kid again. Something I hadn't done in more than a dozen years, and I liked it.

I pulled into the USP Atlanta lot with fifteen minutes to spare. I took my VP9 from its holster and locked it in the glove box, then I exited the Camaro, locked it, and walked toward the main

70

entrance, turning my head now and then, like a kid with a new toy, to take a peek at my new love.

Judge Strange had done me proud. I was expected. One of the deputy wardens was waiting for me. We shook hands, and he ushered me into the interview room. Two minutes later, accompanied by a uniformed guard, ex-congressman Gordon Harper sauntered in. He looked different. It wasn't just what he was wearing—regulation khaki shirt and pants and brown shoes. He'd lost weight: his face was thinner, the skin of his neck was hanging, scrawny. His white hair was thinner, but the piercing blue eyes had lost none of their intensity.

"Harry Starke," he said with a huge smile that reminded me of a hungry alligator. "Well, well, and what a pleasure it is to see you after all this time. What's it been, Harry, two years? Seems longer somehow, but then it would, wouldn't it? Me being in here and all."

I didn't answer. I watched as he sat down opposite me, leaned his elbows on the table, and stared at me, the icy eyes doing their best to drill holes in my face.

I sat back in my chair and stared back at him; his mouth was smiling, but his eyes weren't and, suddenly, I had a flashback to that awful night, two years ago, when Tabitha Willard had jumped to her death from the Walnut Street bridge.

The flashback didn't last but a second or two, but it was enough to remind me that this man, despite the grandfatherly veneer, was one of the evilest men I'd ever had the misfortune to meet.

He continued to smile at me across the four feet of steel and laminate that separated us as he continued, "And to what do I owe this great honor, and on a non-visiting day, no less? Must be something extraordinarily important, I think. All is well with you and yours, I hope," and damned if the man didn't wink at me.

"I heard you got married. Amanda Cole, right? Lovely woman, beautiful. What the hell did she see in you, I wonder? And she's doing well... I hope?" He cocked his head to one side. The inference was obvious.

Right then and there, I could have punched him in the middle of his smug face. He'd barely even sat down, and I had yet to say a word, but he'd already managed to confirm what we'd been thinking.

I shook my head, "Same old Little Billy," I said. "She's doing well. Very well." I folded my arms and stared at him. He stared back at me through half-closed eyes. He looked like a cobra readying to strike.

"So what do you want, Starke?" he asked, the smile was gone, his voice a low growl. "I don't have all day. Things to do people to see. You know how it is."

"Sarcasm doesn't become you, Harper. It never did, and it doesn't now, but I'm not here to get into a pissing match with you. I'm here to tell you to call off your dog."

He pursed his lips, frowned, tilted his head again, looked puzzled and said, "Dog? What dog? What are you talking about?"

"You know what. You put a contract out on me. Cancel it, or I'll have you canceled."

"A contract?" he said, with mock disbelief. "Now there's an idea. Why the hell didn't I think of that? Hmmm. Sounds like a plan," he said, his eyebrows raised.

"Listen, Billy. I know what you're doing, and I know why. I know you blame me for what happened to you, but you chose to do what you did, and that's why you're in here; not because of me. You have only yourself to blame for that."

He gave me the alligator smile but said nothing.

"I'm sorry about Kathryn and her husband too, but that was self-defense; she shot me first. I had no choice."

His hands were clasped tightly together, squeezing, the knuckles turned white, his lips were a tight, thin line; his eyes… narrow slits filled with hate, and then he seemed to relax, a little.

"Of course you didn't, Harry. By the way," he nodded toward my wrist, "are you still wearing that fancy watch?"

He was referring to a sophisticated instrument I'd been given by the Secret Service a couple of years ago when he'd been trying to coerce a United States senator. I'd used it to record sound and video of a conversation we'd had in his office; the recording was used as part of the evidence that put him away.

"No. And I'm not wired either. What's said here, stays here."

"Good." He lowered his head so that his lips couldn't be seen by the security cameras, looked up at me through his eyelashes, and said, in a voice that was barely above a whisper, "Because you're a dead man, Starke. You have been since you killed Kathryn; you just didn't know it. Now you do. But first, I'm going to make you suffer. Do you know what it's like to lose a daughter? No, of course you don't... but you will. First that fancy bitch you married, and then... Well, we'll see. By the time it gets to be your turn, you'll know exactly what it's like, to hurt so bad your guts cramp and your head feels like it's full of concrete and about to burst wide open, to not sleep at night... to... to, well, I only wish I could be there to see it, but just knowing will be enough." He leaned back in his chair, folded his arms, and smiled at me; it was a look of pure evil.

Now I have to admit that he'd gotten to me, just a little. I was used to threats from people I'd put away, but I knew Harper better than most, and I also knew that he *never* made idle threats. I'd been worried before, but now it moved to a higher level. He was watching me, looking for a reaction. I sure as hell wasn't going to give him one, so I leaned back too, and I smiled back at him.

"D'you really think I'm going to sit back and let you do that?" I asked, mildly. "If you do, you don't know me as well as you think you do."

"I know you well enough, Starke. Yes, I do know how good you are, but you know what?" He leaned forward again so that the cameras couldn't see his face, and then whispered, "I found somebody better. Your days are numbered, and so are those of that fancy whore you married. Enjoy them while you can, both of you, if you can."

I nodded, "I hear you, Harper. Now you listen to me." I too leaned forward until there was only a foot or so between our eyes, lowered my head, and then said so that only he could hear, "You put an end to this vendetta, and you do it today. If you don't, it will be you that dies. You think you're safe in here?" I asked, slowly shaking my head. "You're not! One more incident; one more attack on my family or friends, and I'll have you put down like the mangy dog you are. That's not a threat, Billy; that's a promise."

He leaned back in his chair, a twisted grin on his face He was trying hard not to show it, but I'd gotten to him.

"We'll see," he said, rising to his feet. "Have a good day, Harry... Oh, and do give Amanda my best, won't you?" Then he turned and walked to the door, leaving me, still seated at the table, staring at his back.

"*Harper!*" I called after him. He ignored me, "Remember what I said; call off your dog."

He stopped by the door, the guard at his side, then turned and said, "My dog died a year ago, Starke!"

And then he was gone. *Who the hell won that one, I wonder?*

Chapter 8
Wednesday, July 12, 3:30pm

It was a slow ride out of Atlanta that afternoon. I hit the road right in the middle of rush hour. Even so, I remember little of the ninety minutes it took for me to get through Marietta. My mind was full of images I didn't like, and couldn't get rid of. Harper was already winning the mind game wars, but I could live with that. It was the contract that occupied my mind. If it had been only me, that wouldn't have been so bad, but this involved Amanda—that had been made only too plain—and God only knew who else—Kate? Bob? Jacque? My staff?

"Damn! Damn! Damn!" I shouted as I hammered the steering wheel with the heels of my fists.

I gripped the wheel so hard the knuckles and backs of my hands turned white. I jammed my foot down on the gas pedal; the Camaro responded like a wounded tiger; the rear end sank, the car leaped forward, the gears shifting quickly and smoothly as it hurtled from seventy to a hundred and twenty-five in less than ten seconds. Three, maybe four, seconds later the HUD was showing one hundred and fifty-six. I was passing other vehicles like they were standing still. It lasted no more than a minute, but it did the trick. Slowly I calmed down, and as I did, so my speed dropped.

I settled the Camaro down to what now seemed an extremely sedate seventy-five miles an hour and flipped on the cruise control—you never know where those Georgia state troopers may be hiding—and settled back. I let the fine leather enfold me, listened to the sound of the tires on the road, and I grinned to myself, *Geez, that's one hell of a way to get rid of the stress. Gonna have to watch it, though. They'd throw away the damn keys they catch me doing one-fifty... Haha, I doubt they could catch me in this puppy.*

It was just after six that evening when I crossed from Georgia into Tennessee. I'd called Amanda when I left the prison and again when I hit the Chattanooga city limit, just to make sure all was well, and it was; Bob was still with her, helping her cook dinner. Then I called the office. Jacque was still there, so I told her I'd stop by. Finally, I called Kate and asked her to join us on the mountain for dinner.

I rolled up to the gate outside my offices on Georgia Avenue, clicked the remote and opened it, parked and joined Jacque inside; much to my displeasure, she was alone, something I expressly ordered not to happen, and that meant any of my staff. I was, however, pleased to see she had the M&P9 on her right hip.

"What are you doing here by yourself, Jacque?" I asked, seating myself on the corner of her desk.

"I wasn't. At least not until you called. Tim and I were just about to leave. I knew you wouldn't be but a few minutes, so I told him to go and that I'd wait for you."

"Jacque," I said, shaking my head. "That ain't gonna get it. It would take less than a minute for someone to barge in here and... and... and..." I didn't finish.

She got the idea, but Jacque being Jacque, dropped into her native Jamaican accent and said, "You tink I'm stupid? I watched Tim close d' gate behind him, and d' front door was already locked..." She smiled and continued, the accent gone. "Harry. Stop worrying. I'm careful, and so are the rest of the staff. Now, what did you want to see me about?"

"Nothing really... Jacque, I've just come from the prison. It's Harper. He's put out a contract on me. He admitted it. He also said he wanted me to know what it was like to lose someone I loved. He mentioned Amanda specifically, but I'd bet my ass that we're all in danger. We can't drop our guard; not even for a minute. We stay together. We keep the doors locked at all times, and... why the hell aren't you wearing a vest like I asked? Are Tim and the others wearing them?"

She turned around and picked up a black, Spider vest, held it out for me to see, and then

79

said, "I had it on, ready to leave, but then you called, and I took it off again. I can't wear the damn thing all the time, Harry. It's not comfortable, and you're not wearing yours either. Why the hell not?"

She had me there, and I had no answer; In my hurry to get to the dealership, I'd left it at home.

"Okay," I said, sheepishly, "you got me. From now on, I'll do better. Listen, all I wanted was to see you, just to make sure all was well. Is it?"

"Yes, it is. It's been a relatively quiet day. Now, if you don't mind, I need to get home to Wendy."

I nodded. Wendy is her life partner. "Okay, so would you two like to join us for dinner? Bob and Kate will be there."

"I'd like to, but I won't unless you insist. I'd like to keep Wendy out of all this. She knows what's happened, and she's worried sick, so the less she knows, the better..." she hesitated, "I think. Oh hell, Harry. Do we have to?"

"No, of course not, but stay indoors. Don't open it for anyone. If you need me, call, immediately. You hear?"

She did, and with that, she slipped into the Spider and together we walked out into what was supposed to be a secure parking lot and locked the side door behind her. I say *supposed* to be secure because the damned gate was wide open and there was a small, yellow and black smiley face stuck smack dab in the center of the driver's side of the Camaro's windshield. *Christ! I could have sworn I closed the damn thing; I know I did.*

I looked at Jacque. She just shook her head and shrugged. She didn't say a word; she didn't have to, I knew exactly what she was thinking, and I didn't blame her after the conversation we'd just had. I was going to have to do better, a lot better.

I told her goodnight and watched as she drove out of the lot onto Georgia and turned right, then I peeled the sticker off the windshield, got into the car and stuck it gently on the back seat, hit the starter and followed her out onto the street. I stopped the car, clicked the remote and watched as the gate rolled shut, then I got out of the car and checked the electronic lock; all was good. Involuntarily, I glanced up at the three security cameras on the top of the building—there were three more on the far side of the lot. I knew they were on; they always were, even when the offices were open. Tim had even installed facial recognition software into the system—that's one of the perks of having your own geek—not that we'd ever used it… and then I had a thought, *I need to go back in and check the monitors. Maybe…*

I reopened the gate, deactivated the alarm system and went back inside. I clicked the mouse and brought up the multiple screens. I needed to check only the last twenty minutes or so.

I could see that the gate was, indeed, closed, *Yep, I knew I'd closed that sucker.* I watched the gate for maybe five minutes after I'd reentered the building, and then it happened. The damned thing began to roll back, and even before it was fully open, a person wearing jeans and a lightweight yellow hoodie slipped inside, walked quickly to the Camaro, slapped the yellow sticker on the windshield, turned and was gone: five, ten seconds at the most. I ran the section of video several times, but whoever it was, was giving nothing away. The person was wearing sneakers, was maybe five-eight or nine tall... ah, maybe five-ten—It was hard to tell from that angle—medium build, nimble, face covered. I couldn't tell if it was a man or a woman. It could have been a young man. On the other hand, it could easily have been a woman.

I froze the screen and sat back in my seat. I steepled my fingers and put them to my chin, and I stared down at what little I could see of the figure. I must have sat like that for five minutes, maybe more, staring at the screen, before I finally shook my head and rose to my feet.

Back in the car, I thought about my visit with Harper, and what he'd said, *"...but you know what? I found somebody better."*

Maybe he has... I thought as I thumbed the starter button. *Maybe... he... has!*

Chapter 9
Wednesday, July 12, Evening

I parked the beast outside the garage, closed the gate, and was just about to enter through the side door when I was met by Amanda and Bob. They'd heard the gate open and couldn't wait.

"What the hell is that?" Bob asked.

"Oh my God, Harry. What have you done?" Amanda looked at the "beast," wide-eyed.

"It a Camaro ZL1. Like it?"

"Like it? I love it, but isn't it a tad too much?" She walked slowly around it, peered in through the driver side window, opened the door, slipped inside and grabbed the wheel.

"Hah!" Bob said. "You comin' down with midlife crisis? You're gonna let me drive it, Harry, right?"

"Could be," I said as I leaned on the driver's side door and watched as she caressed the wheel. "Let's go inside; I need a drink, okay?" I took a step back and held the door for her.

"Where did you get this?" she asked as she climbed out of the car, the smiley face stuck to her fingertip.

"Drink first, story later. Okay?"

They followed me into the kitchen and Amanda poured me a very large measure of Laphroaig. Kate had not yet arrived.

"Look," I said, stripping off my coat and shoulder rig and hanging them on the back of one of the kitchen bar stools. "I'll explain about the sticker later. Right now I need a shower in the worst way, and a drink—thank you, my love." I saluted her with it and then sipped the fiery golden liquid and breathed in the heavenly, smoky aroma. *Oh, how sweet it is!*

"So," I continued, "Why don't I get in the shower, change clothes, and by that time Kate should be here. We can talk about the car, the sticker, and whatever else has happened, over dinner, or after, depending on how I feel, yeah?"

They both agreed, and I left them to it, heading for the bathroom and a long, very hot shower—I did, of course, take my glass with me.

Twenty minutes later, fully refreshed and wearing shorts, a T and a pair of Sperry's, I returned to the dining room, ready to face the evening, dinner, and what promised to be a long discussion. Kate, dressed in black shorts and a white top, had arrived and was seated at the table nursing a gin and tonic; Bob was sucking on a Bud, and Amanda was drinking something red. As soon as I entered the room, she stated that dinner was ready and we should eat before it got cold. And we did.

We ate, for the most part, in silence, but it was an uneasy silence. My head was full of Harper and the implications of what he'd said. Yeah, I was worried, I now knew for sure that we, all of us, were in danger. Out there somewhere, a shadowy figure was plotting my demise, and if Harper was to be believed, Amanda's too, and there was absolutely nothing I could do about it.

I laid down my knife and fork, grabbed my half-empty glass of Chardonnay, shoved my chair back, stood up and went to look out of the window; I was wondering where to begin. All three knew me well enough to know what was going on in my head, and they sat quietly, waiting. Finally, I returned to the table and said, "We can't talk in here. Grab your drinks and let's go out on the patio."

"You sure?" Bob asked, pointedly.

"Yes, we'll use the table by the wall; should be safe enough." *Geez, I hope it is.*

I went into the kitchen, opened one of the drawers and took out the small ZipLock sandwich baggie I'd placed there the night before when we'd returned from the Sorbonne. Then I joined the others outside at the octagonal teak table under the six-foot high stone wall, but I didn't sit. I couldn't. Not yet. I was antsy as hell.

It was dusk. The air was cool, but the concrete underfoot was still warm from the heat of the daytime sun. A full moon, like a huge silver dollar, hung low over the horizon. The lights of the city were already on, and the great river was a meandering ribbon of shimmering silver.

Any other time, we'd have been enjoying the view, swimming, enjoying each other's company, but not this night. Glass in hand, I walked the perimeter wall, around the south end of the pool, and then the east wall of the patio where I stopped and gazed out over the terraced gardens looking for… well, you know. The air was still; all was quiet, which was unusual, didn't feel right. Many a time I'd go out and sit on the wall, at the same spot where I was right at that moment, and listen to the creatures of the night, but not now; the silence was almost palpable, and the hair on the back of my neck began to prickle. *Is somebody out there? Am I being watched? What if… Damn it, Harry. Quit it. You're letting her get to you. You're letting her win… Is it a her? Kate thinks so. Could be. Why not?*

"Harry!" Amanda's shout startled me back to reality. "Come back, *please!*" And I did.

I sat down at the table, sipped on my drink, and took a deep breath,

"Okay, about the car," I said. "Amanda and I talked about it this morning. The Maxima had become a liability. I needed to get rid of it."

I laid the sandwich bag down on the tabletop; the yellow face smiled up through the plastic. The smile somehow now looked more malicious than happy.

"That," I reached over and tapped the baggie with my finger, "was stuck on the Maxima's windshield when we left here last night. I didn't mention it then because... well... I just didn't; I just didn't want to deal with it, not then.

"The another one—the one Amanda found in the Camaro...Well, I'll get to that in a minute. So anyway, before I headed out this morning, I called Lennie at Mountain View Chevy, and I traded the Maxima for the Camaro; then I headed to Atlanta.

"I'm not sure if Harper was expecting me, but he sure as hell wasn't surprised to see me. He was... well, he was Harper: arrogant, belligerent, cocksure of himself, and in a couple of sentences he made sure I had no doubt that he, or someone working for him, has hired someone... to..." *Oh shit!*

"It's okay, Amanda," the look on her face was one of utter horror. "We'll get through it..." I almost bit my tongue, but it had to be said, "*Now* will you go somewhere safe, *please*?"

"I. Will. Not!"

I sighed, shook my head, opened my mouth to speak, then closed it again, picked up my wine glass, and poured what was left of the contents down my throat.

I got up again, went inside to the bar—I needed something stronger—and poured myself a large scotch.

I returned to the patio and spent the next several minutes giving them a somewhat shortened version of my conversation with Harper. I hit all the highlights, and when I finished, I sat back and waited. The mood around the table that night was, to say the least, bleak

"So. Any thoughts... anybody?" I asked as I looked at them each in turn.

"This is not good, Harry," Bob said, quietly, shaking his head slowly.

"Hah! You can say that again. And there's more," I said. "That second sticker: switching cars didn't work. Not for a minute. I stopped by the office on the way home, to have a word with Jacque. When we left, I found it stuck on the Camaro windshield. What did you do with it, by the way?" I asked Amanda.

"It's in the kitchen. In another of those bags."

"You forgot to close the gate, didn't you?" Kate asked.

I shook my head, "At first, I thought that I must have because it was wide open. But when I went back inside and checked the security footage; I'd closed it alright. Someone else opened it. He, or she—it's not possible to tell which—is on the tape, but you can't see the face: the head's covered and the angle's bad. Whoever it was, must have cloned the remote's frequency, and that means he had to be close, very close.

"It took him less than ten seconds to get in and be gone again.

"Kate, we need to get those smileys to Mike Willis for processing. I haven't touched the surfaces, just a small portion of the sticky on the back of them." I looked at Amanda. She shook her head. I shrugged, "He has our prints anyway, and I doubt very much he'll find anything, but you never know."

"I'll drop them off on my way home."

"Good," I looked around the table, "Okay. So, what do we know?"

"It's a woman," Kate said.

"Man," Bob said.

Amanda said nothing.

"Whatever," I said, "but one thing we now know for sure: whoever it is, is watching my every move, maybe all of us. Changing cars sure as hell didn't throw him off. He must have been here when I left this morning, followed me to Mountain View. If so, he's good; I didn't spot a tail. Then again, I called Lennie before I left so it could be that the house is bugged. I'll call Tim first thing in the morning and have him screen the offices, the cars, and this house. If there are bugs, he'll find them. If not... well."

"So what are we going to do?" Bob asked. "We can't just sit around and wait to get knocked off. We have to find this son of a bitch, and stop him, quick."

Kate was staring at the table shaking her head, "How the hell do we do that, Bob? We know absolutely nothing about him, or her. Talk about hunting for a shadow in the dark."

"Well, we know that Harper is behind it," I said. "He admitted as much to me, which means he knows who it is and where he is. He's not gonna tell us, though; that's for sure. But think about it. He didn't do the hiring, now did he? He couldn't have, not where he is. So that begs the question, who the hell did? If we can figure that out, we might have a shot at it. I'm thinking Shady Tree. Yeah?"

Bob nodded, but I could see his mind was elsewhere.

"What, Bob?" I asked.

He looked me in the eye and said, "You know what my answer to it is. We have to cut the head off the snake… That's Harper. We've got to put him away, permanently."

I smiled at him and shook my head. I well knew that if ever he was given the chance, he wouldn't hesitate; he'd done it before.

"It's not gonna happen, Bob. No! Don't go there. I know you could get it done, even while he's inside, but we're not going to join him in the gutter. We need to find the contractor; put him away."

"You can't be serious, Harry," Bob said. "He's out to kill you. He's got to be stopped. Look, all it will take is a phone call. I can do that. You don't even need to know about it."

"I already do. You just told me."

"But it's not just you we're talking about, now is it?" he asked. "It's Amanda," he looked at her, "and God only knows who else he's targeted. Come on, Harry, we know he's playing games with us—the shot at Amanda, the smiley faces— mind games. That's what he's playing, and right now he's winning. And... sooner or later, the games will stop, and somebody will die."

He paused, looked me in the eye, then said, "Harry, even if we find him, and even if we stop him, it won't stop Harper; you know that. He'll just hire another killer, and then another, until sooner or later... one of them gets lucky. You want her," he nodded in Amanda's direction, "to get hurt, or worse? What if it's Jacque, or Tim, for Christ's sake? You gonna be able to live with that? I sure as hell know I couldn't."

It was one of the longest speeches I'd ever heard him make, and he was right. I wouldn't be able to live with myself, but nor could I live with myself if I allowed him to do what he was proposing.

I shook my head, "Let's try it my way first, okay?"

He simply folded his arms, leaned back in his chair, and glared at me. I didn't know what he was thinking, but I was sure as hell I wouldn't have liked it.

He was also right about the mind games. He, the contractor, if it was a he, already had me constantly looking over my shoulder—hell, I'd watched my rearview mirror all the way home from the office—and I daren't leave Amanda alone, not even for a minute. I looked at her, reached out and took her hand, and tried one more time.

"Geez, Girl, I wish you'd do as I ask and leave until this mess is over…"

She didn't answer; she just slowly shook her head.

"Kate, I don't think you…" I turned and looked at her.

"Don't even go there, Harry. I'm in it until it's finished, one way or another. It's too late now anyway. If they're watching you, they know about us, all of us, and that means the people who work for you too. This is one hell of a mess. If she—yeah, I told you; I think it's a woman—if she's planning to do what I think she is, Bob's right. Before she gets around to you, people are going to die; your people… I can look after myself. So can Bob, yeah, and so can you, but what about

92

Amanda, Jacque, Tim, and the others? They're not trained for situations like this: they're going to be sitting ducks."

Amanda shuddered; I squeezed her hand.

"You're right, Kate, but other than send them all off out of the country, what do I do? This one," I glanced at Amanda, "and Jacque won't go. Tim... maybe, and the others. Shit!"

"Damn it, Harry," Bob growled. "You make 'em go."

"How? You want me to carry them kicking and screaming onto the plane?"

"If you have to, yeah! Hell, I'll do it."

I shook my head. Was I frustrated? Hell yes! Were they right? Of course they were, but they didn't know Amanda like I did. She'd fight teeth and claw, and so would Jacque.

"You're right, Bob," I said. I looked at him. There was a glint in his eye and a tight smile on his lips.

"No, no," I said. "What I mean is, we need to find this son of a bitch, and fast, but how?"

"Shady," Kate said. "If we can find him..."

I nodded, "I wonder if Benny's had any luck."

I took my iPhone from my shorts pocket and punched the speed dial for the Sorbonne, then I looked at my watch. Hell, they weren't even open yet.

"Hello?"

"Hey, Laura, it's Harry. Is he there?"

"No. He's out. Said he was on a mission for you. He wouldn't say what it was. Can I help?"

"No, but thanks. When will he be back; do you know?"

"He shouldn't be more than an hour, I hope. I'll have him call you?"

"I'll try his cell, but yeah. If I don't get hold of him, have him call me, as soon as he comes in, Laura, and thanks." I disconnected, went to the contacts screen on my phone, found the number and hit call: no answer.

Damn. I need him to get his ass out of his hands and find Lester Tree.

My patience was running thin, or maybe it was stress. Whatever.

"Okay, so let's think about this a little more," I said. "Put yourselves in this... this, contractor's place. You need to watch your prey, right? This location is a little out of the way, right? And it's kind of isolated. A car parked anywhere here on Brow would stick out like a sore thumb, so that wouldn't be an option. Have either of you seen anything out of the ordinary?"

Neither Amanda or Bob had. Kate had arrived after I did and, so she said, there were no cars parked along the road, at least none that she'd seen, just a hiker, a girl, a young kid.

"That's it," I said. "Has to be. Where was she?" I jumped to my feet.

"Hold on, Harry. I told you, she was just a kid, a student maybe, eighteen or nineteen, no more than that. She was sitting on the wall, down the road fifty or sixty yards away."

I grabbed a chair, set it against the wall, climbed up on it, looked over the top, both ways: nothing, no one. I climbed down and returned to my seat.

"Well?" Kate asked.

I shook my head, "I couldn't see anyone, but that doesn't mean... So what, then?" I asked. "Someone creeping about down there, on foot, maybe?" I waved a hand in the direction of the gardens. "That hardly seems likely. What would you do, Kate, if you wanted to stay under the radar? You'd dress and act like a tourist, or a damned hiker, right?" I asked; the inference was obvious. She shrugged.

And so it went on, for at least another hour. We talked it to death, and we came up with nothing. We were at a dead end. The only thing we could think of that made any sense was that we had to find Shady Tree. Until then, we had to lay low, all of us.

I asked Amanda to prepare the guest room for Kate and Bob, and then I made calls to all my people. I told them that I'd closed the business and that they were to stay home, sit tight and out of sight until further notice. That didn't go down too well, and I had a nasty feeling it wouldn't happen either. I wasn't too sure what good it would do anyway, but it was a whole lot better, at least in my mind, than doing nothing and virtually handing the contractor his victims on a silver platter.

My clients? My ongoing cases? I asked Jacque to call everyone and tell them we had an emergency and that everything was on hold until further notice. It would piss a lot of them off, but what the hell.

My last call had been to Tim. I told him I'd pick him up first thing in the morning. I also told him to stay put until I got there, and to keep a sharp eye out for anything out of the ordinary. And that, I knew, was also a waste of breath. Tim lived in a world way beyond this one. I'd lost count of the number of times he'd almost gotten killed jaywalking, away with the birds, outside the offices on Georgia Avenue. He'd be on the sidewalk one minute, and in the middle of the street, in traffic, the next, God love him.

Chapter 10
Thursday, July 13, 8am

It was just after eight that following morning when I arrived at Tim's home on Brynwood Drive in Hixson. Sam, his girlfriend, had already left for work and he was waiting for me. Tim is my computer guy, a geek in every sense of the word: tall, skinny, weighs less than 150 pounds, glasses, twenty-seven years old, looks sixteen, speaks (well, sort of) and writes fluent binary, and once he starts talking it's almost impossible to shut him up. Even worse is that most of the time nobody can understand what the hell he's talking about. But he's the best there is, and I wouldn't swap him, not even for Amanda... Er, I take that back.

"I have coffee ready," he said, shoving his glasses up the bridge of his nose. "You want some?"

I looked at my watch, hesitated, nodded, and followed him into the kitchen.

"So. What's this all about?" he asked as he handed me a large mug of something that vaguely resembled black coffee. I suspected it tasted even worse than it looked, but I made like I was happy and sipped on the steaming liquid. I was right: I've tasted better paint stripper.

"I think we have a big problem, Tim. I think we've been bugged. This... this person that Harper hired seems to know my every move. I'm sure he knows I'm here right now, so…"

He grabbed my arm with his hand and put his fingers to his lips with the other. I took the hint and stopped talking. He nodded, put his hand to his ear as if he had a phone in it, and then held out his other hand and flipped his fingers; he wanted me to give him something. *What the hell?*

"What makes you think that?" he asked, his finger at his lips, warning me to be careful.

"I found something on my new car yesterday that shouldn't have been there. Nobody knew I had it… I don't know, Tim; it's just a feeling."

It wasn't—just a feeling—it was a whole lot more than just a feeling, but I didn't know what he, Tim, was up to, or what he wanted me to say. So I figured I'd say as little as possible, and play along with him.

He nodded, came close and whispered in my ear, "Give me your phone. Play along with me."

I handed it to him,

"You want me to look for bugs?" he asked. "That's simple enough. Shouldn't take but a few minutes. I need to get ahold of some equipment, though." Again, he held his finger to his lips.

I raised my eyebrows. The boy had more equipment than Microsoft.

"You think…"

"You're the boss," he said, interrupting me.

I shrugged and nodded, still not understanding what he was getting at.

"Can you do that?" I asked, playing along.

"Yes, I think so. Let's go to my den, and I'll make a couple of calls, yeah? Cool. Hey. You want to see the new gear you bought for me, Mr. Starke?" he asked, nodding hugely, his eyes wide.

"Sure," I said. "How much have you cost me this time?"

"Cool. You'll wanna take off your jacket," he said. "It's kinda warm back there, what with the electronics, an' all."

"Yeah, right," I said, beginning to see where he was going. Warm as it was, I was wearing a lightweight golf jacket over the Spider vest and the VP9 on my belt.

"You can put it on the back of that chair." He was grinning like a fool.

"C'mon. My den—Sam calls it my lair—is through here; follow me." I knew that!

And he picked up his coffee and walked out of the kitchen—leaving my phone on the table. I followed him down the hall and into his inner sanctum. I'd been in there before, but I'd never gotten used to the ethereal feeling of the room. But for a small desk lamp, and the light of a half dozen huge computer screens, the room was dark.

"Okay," he said, closing the door. "That should do it. This room is soundproof. Grab a seat. When did you last backup your phone? I'm going to need to reset it to its original factory settings."

"It backs up automatically… What's going on, Tim? Is something wrong with my phone?"

He sighed, shook his head, and with his forefinger, shoved his glasses even farther up the bridge of his nose.

"I don't know, maybe. I doubt very much you, we've been bugged. Today's smartphone is the ultimate spy tool. They don't need to bug anything these days," he said as he sipped on his coffee. "All they need is a spy app on one or all of our iPhones or Androids and the phone numbers, and they can do just about anything from call monitoring to recording and even listening to a conversation."

I knew some of that of course, but I had a feeling I was about to learn a whole lot more.

"So tell me," he said. "What makes you think someone is listening in?"

So I did, I told him what had happened over the last two days. He listened carefully, without interrupting me, a first for him,

"Okay," he said. "Most of it could be just coincidence… the car, however… Who knew what you were planning?"

"No one! No one could have known, other than Amanda, that I was planning to trade it. I didn't say anything to anyone, and I know she didn't. I

100

called Lennie at Mountain View Chevy just before I left the house yesterday morning. It took me less than twenty minutes to get there, and I was on the road to Atlanta less than ten minutes after that; no one could have known about it."

"Well someone obviously did, and that could have been the phone call you made to the dealership. Someone was listening; had to be."

"How? I have my phone with me all the time. I never go anywhere without it." *Oh hell. Big mistake. Now I'll not be able to stop him.*

"There are a couple of ways… well, more than a couple, but the most likely would be an app downloaded to the phone. Failing that, they could be using a Stingray cell tower simulator. If there's a Stingray somewhere, we have to find it. They will be operating a man in the middle attack. The device acts as a cell tower. All smartphones are programmed to access the nearest tower, and if there's a simulator close by, that would be the one, the man in the middle. A Stingray is the most likely—the police have them, though they're not supposed to use them. It would need a power supply and a safe location, so I doubt that's it. More likely what we have here is a spyware app that's been downloaded to one or more of the phones, Flexispy, or some such."

And I'd heard of such spyware too, and even the Stingray, but I'd never figured I'd ever run into it, not out here in the sticks. Chattanooga's a small city.

I nodded, and he continued, "If Flexispy has been installed on your iPhone—and that's the route I would go—the person doing the spying can remotely operate your phone. Hell, they can take it over, if they want to. They can turn on the microphone and listen to conversations; turn on the camera, make calls, read your texts, send texts from it, anything you can do. He could do it remotely, even when you think it's turned off, and you'd never know it was happening. Not only that, when you make a call, the spy can receive an alert, make a call to your number, and listen in on the conversation."

"No shit?"

"Oh yeah! And it gets worse. They have access to all of your sensitive information: user names, passwords, account numbers... everything. My guess is, that's exactly what we have here. Somehow, your spy has been able to physically access your phone and download the Flexispy app—or whatever app it might be. It would take less than a couple of minutes to do it, but he would have had to get his hands on the actual phone." He leaned back in his chair and watched my face. I could almost hear the wheels turning inside his head.

"We have to assume," he continued, "that all of our phones are compromised but in particular yours and Amanda's. There's an easy and quick fix, though. I can reset the phones back to the factory setting. If it's an app like, say, Flexispy, that will fix it. If it's something else; if something was downloaded remotely, that would be another story. I could reset it, but there would be nothing to stop them from doing it again, just as soon as I'd wiped it clean. Your call, Boss. What do you want me to do?"

"Let me think about it for a minute." I thought and then said, "Suppose you did wipe them clean. That would give the game away, let them know we're onto them, right?"

He nodded.

"You're sure it's an app?"

"No. I'm not, but it's the most likely solution."

"Can you dig inside the phone software and find it?"

"Not without subjecting it to some very sophisticated software, which I don't have; we've never needed it before. I could write it, I think, but that would take time, a lot of time… or I could buy it. I know a couple of guys…"

I shook my head. I had an idea.

"How about this?" I asked. "Suppose we leave them, all of them, just as they are?"

He raised his eyebrows, nodded, and waited for me to continue.

"If we did that, we could achieve several things, I think. First, whoever this is would think they were in the clear, right?"

"Oh boy," he said, shaking his head. "Yeah, but you'd need to be very careful to pull it off. If you stop making calls, he'll know something's wrong."

"Yeah, I know, but that could be worked around. Second, we'd be able to feed him disinformation, maybe draw him out."

"Harry, we have no idea what we're up against. First, there are a lot of people that would be involved: you, Amanda, me, Ronnie, Bob, Jacque… Heather… We'd all have to be watching every word we said whenever a phone is close by. These people aren't fools. They'll pick up on the slightest mistake, forced conversations, acting, they'll know, and then it's us that will be on the hook."

He was right, but… Well, it was hellish risky. Instead of flushing him out, we might just drive him under cover or, worse.

He thought for a moment, then said, "Do you have any idea who might have had access to your phones over the last couple of weeks? Just for a minute or two; that's all it would take. They'd only need to handle it for ten or fifteen seconds: open Safari, punch in the URL, hit download, and it's done. Hell, I leave mine around all over the place. Anyone could get to it. How about you?"

I thought about it. If I had left my phone unattended, I couldn't remember when or where, but it could have happened. Amanda? The same, I supposed, in a café, restaurant, anyplace where they could get at the phone.

"I dunno, Tim. It could have happened... Is there any other way to do it, other than physically handling the phone?"

"Oh yeah. It's possible to do it remotely, but that would require a cell tower simulator or some really sophisticated software—the Russians do it all the time, so do the British, the Israelis, the Chinese... It's not something that's readily available. If that's what we have here, we have a real problem. If that's how it was done, if there is a Stingray out there somewhere, we have to find it. If not, we're screwed. No matter how many times we reset the phones, change the numbers, as soon as you make a call the simulator will get the new information, the new numbers, and we're back where we were..."

"I understand," I said. "So, we need to assume the spy is operating a Stingray and has downloaded the app?"

"That would be the best approach."

"Okay, so here's how we'll play it," I said. "How many burner phones do you have?"

"At the last count, a dozen."

"Good. I want everyone involved to have one. We'll use those for sensitive communications: anything we don't want our spy to know. The regular phones… we'll keep on using them. We'll just need to be careful what we talk about and what we say. We'll never, and I mean *ne-ver!* talk strategy when one of them is within earshot. I want you to instruct Bob, Jacque and Ronnie as to what we're doing, and to make sure they understand how important it is that they comply, to the letter. Can you do that?"

He nodded.

"Good. I'll handle things with Amanda."

"What about Kate and Lonnie?"

I thought about that, but I really didn't need to; they were in the loop, so they had to be included.

"Yes. Them too. You handle that as well. Oh, and is there any way you can check around the house for one of those simulators?"

"Yes, as soon as you like."

"The sooner the better. We need to know what we're up against. This afternoon, yeah?"

He nodded.

"Good! Now, give me two of the burners, and let's get back to the kitchen and start this thing rolling. As soon as I'm gone, go somewhere quiet, use one of the burners and call everyone… no… no, don't do that. Go visit them all in person. Use written notes to tell 'em to keep quiet and listen.

Get them away from their phones, just the way you did me—good work, by the way." He grinned and shoved his glasses up the bridge of his nose. "Fill them in on what's going on, give them each a burner, and explain the plan. Got it?"

"Got it!"

"Good. Now I need to go to the house and talk to Amanda, and then… well, I need to think… So! Okay. Let's go back to the kitchen. This time, you play along with me."

He grinned and nodded, "Go for it!"

As we walked back into the kitchen I started talking, playing like we'd been discussing possible electronic bugs.

"Okay. I need to get out of here. Go get the equipment you need and then go sweep the office. You can do that now, right? Good. If you find anything, I want to know right away, and I'll expect you up at the house this afternoon. If the house is bugged, I want to know that too. Be careful, Tim."

He grinned, nodded, and winked, and I put on my jacket, picked my iPhone gently up off the table, slipped it into my pocket, and left him standing at the door, smiling. *Geez, nothing ever seems to worry that boy.*

It was when I was back in my car that I had another thought: my father. He wouldn't be able to make his calls to me. *Damn! I gotta fix that.*

I hit the starter, turned on some music, and exited the car leaving my iPhone on the passenger side seat.

I knew August wouldn't answer a number he didn't know so I couldn't call him using the burner phone. Instead, I called Leo Martan. I gave him the new number and asked him to have August call me, then I hung up, leaned against the Camaro and waited.

Five minutes later, the burner warbled. I explained the situation. He listened without comment. I told him not to call me and that I would call him. He wasn't happy about it, but that's how we left it, and he had my new number if he needed it.

Chapter 11
Thursday, July 13, 10am

I drove slowly back to the house that morning. The inside of my head was a maelstrom. I kept glancing down at the iPhone on the passenger seat. The damned thing looked benign enough, but if what Tim had told me was true, it was now only slightly less dangerous that a stick of dynamite. My mind was in a whirl. Already I was beginning to see problems with my plan. *Christ! Benny! I need to head him off at the pass.*

I pulled into the parking lot of the Publix store at the bottom of the mountain, left the iPhone in the car, and went inside. I found a quiet spot among the shelves, took the burner phone from my pocket, and called him.

"Yeah. Who is this?"

"Benny. It's me, Harry."

"Hey, Harry. What gives. You got a new phone? I didn't recognize the number."

"Yes, something like that. Listen. Have you found him yet?"

"No, but I'm thinking I might have something for you this afternoon."

"For God's sake, Benny. Don't spook him. I need him in the worst way."

"No probs, Harry. I sure as hell ain't gonna talk to 'im myself."

"Good. Now listen and listen good. *Do not call me on my old number… EVER.* You got it? In fact, *don't call me at all.* I'll call you. Understand?"

"Yeah, yeah, Harry. What's wrong? What's goin' on?"

"We think our phones have been hacked. So are you sure you understand what I'm telling you: don't call me, I'll call you, right?"

"Okay, okay, Harry. I got it. But what if I find something out?"

Sheesh! What if he finds something out? I thought. *What if he finds something out?*

"When do you think you'll know something?"

"Hell, Harry. How should I know? This afternoon, maybe… early this evening. I dunno, do I?"

"Okay, here's what we'll do. If you absolutely need to call, use this number, but only in an emergency. Let it ring two times and then hang up, and I'll call you back. Other than that, I'll call you at five-thirty. You be waiting. Yeah?"

"I can do that, yeah."

"Good. Now I gotta go. No calls, other than in an emergency right?"

"I hear yuh: no calls. I won't call yuh."

"Right, bye," and I disconnected the call, grabbed a bottle of wine as I passed the shelf—what the hell it was I had no idea—I paid for it and walked across the lot to the car.

I started up Ochs Highway and called Amanda, on the iPhone.

"Hey," I said, not giving her a chance to speak. "I'm almost home. I grabbed a bottle of red at Publix. Look, I can't talk I'm on Ochs, on the bends, and I can barely keep this damned car on the road. See you in a couple of minutes." And I disconnected, grinning to myself. That call explained my stop, and I'd managed to come up with a good reason why I couldn't talk. If someone *was* listening, I'd covered my ass, I hoped.

I parked the car in the garage, closed the iron gates, and went through into the kitchen. Amanda was at the window.

"Hey you," I said, as I walked quickly to her. "Come 'ere. I need a hug in the worst way."

"Okay… oh…"

I grabbed her and pulled her close, cutting off any chance that she might have said something compromising.

"Do not say anything," I whispered in her ear. "Where's your phone? Point to it."

She did. It was on the breakfast bar.

"Geez, I love you," I said, loud enough for anyone listening to hear. "Have you had a good morning? Yeah? Me too. Tim's coming by later, but right now, I'd like to swim. How about you?" I asked, nodding vigorously.

"Oooh," she said, playing along. "That would be lovely, but first," she glanced at her phone and smiled, "I need something for my nerves… no, not a drink. You know what I need. I need you to make love to me. Pleeease?"

"What, right now?" I said, playing to the phone. "It's not even lunchtime yet."

"So?" she said, "Come on. Come *on!*"

"Geez. Can I at least take off my jacket first?"

"Here. Let me get it." And she did. And she threw it at one of the chairs and missed, and I heard the iPhone in the pocket hit the oak floor. *Damn. She's good. That should do the trick.*

I followed her into the bedroom and closed the door.

She swung round, her face white, "The damn phones are bugged, right?"

I heaved a deep breath and nodded, "We don't know for sure. There's no way to tell, but it does seem likely. The problem is, we can't clean them, or discard them. If he's listening, that will tip him off that we know about him and, for now at least, it's better not to do that. If we can pull it off, we can take the lead and feed him misinformation so we'll know what we're doing, but he won't; I hope."

I spent the next fifteen minutes telling her what Tim had told me. And like me, she was not unfamiliar with the problems the convenience of high tech brought with it, especially the smartphone. She just didn't realize the depth and breadth of it. So, I explained about the burner phones and how and when they were to be used, and then I shut the conversation down. It was too damned depressing to keep on keeping on, worrying it to death and getting nowhere.

We were seated together on the bed, but neither of us had any desire to take advantage of the moment. I stood up and looked down at her. She looked like a little girl: short skirt, knees together, feet apart, toes pointed inward, chewing on her thumbnail.

She dropped her hand to her lap, looked up at me, and asked, "So what are we going to do? We can't live like this forever… in fear. You have to do something, Harry."

"You're right. I do, and I intend to, but what? I have to find this person, and the only way I can see to do that is to find out who and where he is. As far as I know, only two people know that: Harper and whoever he used to do the hiring."

I looked at my watch. We'd been gone for almost a half an hour.

"It's time we were out of here. Any longer will look suspicious. I really would like to swim. We can talk more once we're in the water. You up for it?"

She nodded, "Let me change into a swimsuit; it won't take a minute."

I changed too, and we walked out through the kitchen to the pool, taking our iPhones with us. We placed them on the teak table next to the wall, and I climbed up on it and look up and down East Brow: nothing. Then, together, we slipped, hand in hand, into the pool and swam lazily to the infinity wall, just about as far away from the two phones as we could get. And there, elbows on the edge of the pool, we spent the next hour splashing with our feet, whispering together, and enjoying the view. Although, as I remember it, I looked at it, I sure as hell don't remember *seeing* it. My head was so full of crap I could barely think straight.

I was just about to call it a day and get out of the water when she turned her head toward me, and with her cheek lying on her arm, said, "It might be the only answer, you know; what Bob suggested."

"What? What did he suggest?" I knew damn well what he'd suggested, but I wanted to hear her say it, but she didn't. She just turned away, rested her chin on her arms, and gazed out over the city.

I didn't bother to pursue it. I well knew how scared she was, and scared people say things they don't mean.

114

I put my arm around her, laid my head next to hers, and whispered, "It will be all right."

Somehow, even with my weight on her, she managed to shrug, and right then I knew she didn't believe me.

***

It was after three o'clock that afternoon when Tim arrived, and that in itself presented a problem. If we were being watched, the watcher would know what we were up to. Before I could let him loose with his gadgetry, I needed to think it through; talk to him.

I met him outside the gate. He was still in his car. He pushed open the passenger side door and gestured for me to get in. I did and closed the door.

"Okay, so what's the plan, Tim? You can't go wandering around the neighborhood looking like an out of work water diviner. If we're being watched, you'll give the game away."

He nodded, "That had crossed my mind," he said, dryly. "But I have a plan. See this?" He had a small device in his hand.

"Yeah. What is it?"

"It's a cell tower locator. I have a map of all the towers on the mountain and in the valleys. If there's a bogus tower—a Stingray or some such—anywhere close, this little beauty can find it."

"How? I just told you, you can't go walking around with that thing. If you're seen…"

"I don't have to. There isn't one. I drove up Ochs Highway and then West Brow all the way to Covenant College, and from there back to Point Park. There are two towers there, close to Point Park—those are what your iPhones are detecting—and there's another at Covenant; that's it. I don't have to do anything else. If there was a Stingray operating anywhere close to your house, this baby would have detected it. You're in the clear… except for the phones, that is."

I nodded, "Good job, Tim. You coming in? Amanda has iced tea. Take a load off, yes?"

"No, I don't think so, if you don't mind. I'm supposed to be taking Sam to dinner, and I'd like a few minutes at home to clean myself up. D'you mind?"

"No, of course not. But…"

"Yeah, I know. Just stay off the iPhones, Harry. Use the burners. I doubt the house is bugged, so I think you're safe to use them. But hey, I can run a quick scan to see. Shouldn't take more than ten minutes to check the living room, kitchen and your bedroom. If they're clean, I'd say the rest of the house is too. As to the iPhones… Look, you can always take the batteries out of them, right? That will shut them down completely, but…"

"Yes, please. Run a scan for bugs, if you wouldn't mind. I'd feel a whole lot more comfortable knowing for sure. As to removing the batteries, I'll think about it."

And he did, but he found nothing, much to my relief. Now at least I knew we could talk normally together.

I arranged to meet him, along with the others, at my office the following morning, then I told him goodbye and asked him to call me when he got home, and then I watched him drive away. I worried about that boy. Smart as he was, he paid little attention to what was going on around him, and with what was going on right now that could be the death of him.

Chapter 12
Thursday, July 13, 10pm

I called Benny at five-thirty as arranged; he'd still heard nothing, so I called him again at eight, and yet again ten. Nothing, so I arranged to call him again at nine the next morning. That didn't go down well, not at all. Benny is a creature of the night and usually sleeps until two in the afternoon, sometimes even later. It took several threats of grievous bodily harm at my own hands before he finally agreed.

I put the burner phone in my pants pocket and damned if my iPhone didn't ring. *Benny,* I thought, promising myself that I'd kick his fat ass as soon as I saw him again, but it wasn't. I looked at the screen. It was Kate. *What the…?* It was just after ten o'clock.

"Kate…" I know I must have sounded angry, but she ignored me and interrupted.

"Shut up, Harry, and for Christ's sake listen for once. Ronnie is in Erlanger. He's been shot. Get your ass down here. Now!" And she disconnected, leaving me staring in horror at the phone.

There's no way you'll ever know, no way for me to possibly explain how I felt. Devastated doesn't even begin to describe it. Horrified? Not hardly. I felt sick. I wanted to puke, needed to puke. I felt like I'd been hit by a two-by-four. Yes,

I know. I'm supposed to be one tough son of a bitch, right? Yeah, that's what everybody thinks. It's a persona I'd actively cultivated. But you know what? I'm not that guy, not really, not even a little bit, and that night, I have to admit, was probably one of the worst of my life.

I'd known Ronnie for more than sixteen years, since he'd gotten out of school, in fact. He and Bob were my first two hires when I left the CPD and went into business for myself. He was a quiet, self-deprecating man dedicated to his family, especially to his twelve-year-old son, Mikey; Mikey was autistic... *Son... of... a... He's winning. The sleazy bastard son of a bitch is winning.*

I jumped up off the sofa and cracked my knee on the edge of the coffee table and almost fell head first over it as I rushed to the bedroom, and told Amanda to get dressed, in anything, and quick.

"What? What is it? What's wrong?" She had just gotten out of the shower and was wrapped in a towel,

"For Christ's sake, Amanda, just get dressed. I'll tell you in the car. Where's your goddamn phone?"

"Over there," she pointed, and by now badly frightened. She dropped the towel and ran to the dresser. It took her only minutes to drag on a pair of panties, a T-shirt and jeans. While she did, I grabbed her iPhone—I swear to God, I nearly opened the window and threw it, along with my own, down the mountain, but I didn't. Instead, I held them both close to my lips.

"Okay, you son of a bitch. I know you're listening. Now you can listen to *ME!* I got your message. You went after one of mine; big, *big* mistake. Now I'm coming for you. Harper says you're good. Let me tell you this, you piece of shit: you're not good enough. So take your best shot, and make it count because if you don't, I'm going to tear your goddamn head off and jam it up your ass."

Then I stripped the batteries from both phones and flung them down on the bed. *To hell with you. From now on, you'll know no more than I do.*

I grabbed Amanda's hand and literally dragged her into the garage. I hit the remote for the garage door, the remote to open the gate, and the starter button in that order. Then I reversed the car out onto the street, closed the garage door and the gate, hit the gas pedal and almost smashed the damned car into the stone perimeter wall that surrounds my house and property.

"For God's sake, Harry," Amanda screamed. "Stop it! You'll kill us!"

Only then did I come to my senses. It must have been her screaming. I'd never heard her do that before. I looked across at her. She was hanging onto the strap for dear life. Was she ever scared? Oh yeah, she was scared, and so was I as I saw, out of the corner of my eye, one of those brick-built mailboxes hurtling toward me. I slammed on the brakes, twisted the wheel, and scraped by with less than a coat of paint to spare, and then I truly calmed down, but not completely. I needed to get to the hospital, and nice wasn't the way to do it.

I wasn't watching the clock, but I know I made that trip in less than ten minutes; hell, I know I hit ninety on one section of Broad; damn good job there were no cops about.

I was lucky enough to find a parking spot in the Siskin lot just opposite the hospital Emergency Entrance off Blackford Street. I wasn't too happy about leaving my new baby there, but I didn't have a lot of choice.

We found Kate and Lonnie in the emergency room waiting area. Lonnie was asleep; Kate... well, she wasn't. She saw us as soon as we walked through the doors, and came to meet us.

"Okay," I said—she was still a dozen feet away—"Tell me. How is he? Is he going to be okay?"

She was smiling. *What the hell is there to smile about?* I wondered.

"Yeah, he going to be fine." She was almost laughing.

"What the hell's so funny, Kate? You told me Ronnie had been shot. What..."

"Calm down, Harry. Ronnie... how do I put this? His pride is hurt more than his ass."

"*What?* What the hell are you talking about?"

"Our friendly neighborhood spy shot him in the ass... twice, with a twenty-two."

"Wha... What? How the hell did that happen?"

"He said he went to Walmart; to get some cheese. Apparently, he was bending over the lower shelf—you know, where they keep the big, two-pound blocks of cheddar—and someone walked up behind him and put two in his ass, one in each cheek."

"What the hell is he playing at, Kate? What kind of contract killer pulls stunts like that?"

Before she could answer, a nurse came through the double doors into the waiting area, "You can see him now, Lieutenant... Er... who..."

"It's okay," Kate said. "They're with us."

The woman nodded, held the door for us, and we followed her down a long corridor, into the elevator, and eventually into a room where Ronnie was lying face down on the bed, a white sheet covering his rear end.

"We've removed the bullets. They didn't do much damage. The wounds will be painful for a day or two—we've given him something for that—but we'll need to keep him here overnight to keep an eye on him. The doctor will probably release him sometime tomorrow unless the wounds become infected. Use the call button if you need me." And she left us standing around the bed looking down at him.

"Hey," he said. "Sit the hell down. I can't see you."

We sat. He turned his head toward me and grinned... well, he tried to. It came across as a pained grimace.

"Hiya, Harry," he said, through gritted teeth. "Funny, huh?"

"No, not so funny. How're you feeling, Ronnie?"

"It hurts like hell is how I'm feeling. They gave me some... hell, I don't know what it was. I can barely move my legs."

I leaned forward and patted him on the shoulder. He looked up at me. Yeah, he was hurting. I could see it in his eyes.

"What did the doctor say?"

"He said there wasn't any real damage. He removed the slugs—twenty-two's—and said I wouldn't be able to sit down for a few days. Shit, Harry. I did what you told me. I was wearing a vest under my jacket. I can't believe she shot me in the ass."

"Better than... She? How do you know it was a she? Did you see her?"

"No, I didn't. Well, some. I was bending over the cheese bin... We love that white cheddar... I felt—I didn't hear—someone come up behind me. I started to turn my head. I could see a pair of Adidas sneakers, small, a woman's. Then she said, 'Ronnie?' I said yes, and was already half up when I felt like I'd been kicked in the left side of my ass and stung by a friggin' hornet, both at the same time. Less than a second later, same again, on the other side. I tried to stand up, but by the time I'd turned around she'd gone; no sign of her. By then it was starting to hurt; oh man did it ever hurt. Harry, you have no idea. My ass was literally on fire. I couldn't stand. I went down on my knees, and I was leaking blood like a bucket with a hole in it. I managed to call 911, then I couldn't stand the pain anymore…"

"You didn't hear the gunshots?"

He tried to shake his head, but he was face down on the pillow.

"No, well, I might have; I heard something. I don't remember. If I did, they were very quiet. She must have been using a suppressor."

"Yeah, and that means she also used sub-sonic ammo. A twenty-two; I doubt you would have heard them, even as close as she was, and the sub ammo, low-velocity rounds, is probably the reason the slugs didn't do more damage."

What the hell is she playing at? She could just as easily have put two in the back of his head; killed him, but she didn't. Why not? More games?

"Well," I said, leaning back in my chair. "Geez, Ronnie. I'm glad…" I heaved a sigh and shook my head. "I'm glad you're okay.

"Tell Jean I'll be here to pick you up when you're released tomorrow, see you safely home. Where is she, by the way?"

"She and Mikey are in Tucson. I sent her to stay with her mother. Don't tell her, Harry. Let me do it. Okay? This isn't that bad. I'll be walking out of here tomorrow. There's no need to worry her or Mikey." He twisted his head trying to see me better.

"What about her, though; this… woman?" he asked.

"I don't think you need to worry. It's me she's after." *And Amanda!*

My head spun at the thought. I looked at her. She stared back at me. The look on her face? I can't describe it. The color had drained. She looked pallid; her lips were drawn tight, compressed, a grim line that looked the worse for her lack of makeup, not that she ever wore much, but no lipstick… well, you get the idea.

We talked for a few more minutes, but I could see it was tiring him; it was time to go.

"We have to go, Ronnie, but I'll see you tomorrow, okay? In the meantime, is there anything you need, anything I can get for you?" I stood, patted him lightly on the shoulder.

"No, nothing. Have a good one, Harry. Bye, Amanda. Take care, you hear?"

"Bye, Ronnie," Amanda said as she leaned over and kissed him on the cheek. "Try to get some sleep. You'll feel better in the morning; I'm sure."

He grimaced, turned his head a little, and thanked her.

Outside in the hallway, I spent a few minutes with Kate and Lonnie and arranged to meet them both at my office at ten the following morning. Why? Hell, I had no idea. Just to yak it through for the umpteenth time, I supposed.

We said our goodbyes and Amanda and I left the hospital. As we walked across the road and approached the Camaro, I had a certain and eerie feeling that we were being watched.

I held the car door for Amanda and, while she lowered herself into the seat, I looked around. There were maybe a couple of dozen cars in the lot; none of them seemed to be occupied. Inwardly, I shrugged, walked around the car, and climbed down into the driver's seat. As I did so, I happened to glance out through the passenger side window, just in time to see a black Mini Cooper reverse out of a space some fifty yards on down the lot. It turned and drove slowly away in the other direction, toward Siskin Drive, and out of my line of sight. I started the Camaro, reversed out of my space and followed. By the time I'd reached Siskin, there was no sign of the Mini.

I hadn't mentioned it to Amanda. I didn't want to alarm her; besides, what did I know? So a car pulled out and drove away. Could have been anybody, but I had a deep-seated feeling it wasn't. My so-called second sight—or was it merely intuition—was in overdrive. Paranoia? Probably. I learned during my years at Fairleigh Dickinson University that the line between intuition and paranoia is very thin. I felt exposed and vulnerable, and that wouldn't change until I knew who the hell I was up against.

I said nothing to Amanda about the Mini, or my suspicions, as I headed west on Central Avenue. Ahead, Lookout Mountain was a vast, dark mass, topped with a crown of glittering lights, set against a clear, night sky: stunning.

A few minutes later we were heading up the mountain on Scenic Highway and had just passed over the Incline Railway, about half way up when Amanda turned in her seat and said, "What are we going to do, Harry?"

They were the first words out of her mouth since we'd left the hospital. I knew what she wanted; she wanted some sort of reassurance from me that everything was going to be all right. The trouble was, I didn't know if it would, but I sure as hell couldn't, wouldn't, tell her that.

"I'm going to find this… this… this *woman*, one way or another, and I'm going to stop her."

"You mean you're going to kill her."

That's exactly what I meant. Only I couldn't say that either. It would have scared her to death.

"That's not my intent, but if that's what it takes," I said. I don't like to lie, and especially not to Amanda, but that time I did. I had a feeling that, if she was all Harper had claimed, killing the woman was the only way to stop her from killing me or one or more of us. It was eventually going be either me or her anyway. I wouldn't be given a choice.

Out of the corner of my eye, I saw Amanda nod. She had her hands clasped together around her knees.

"She's good, isn't she, Harry?"

I nodded but said nothing.

"Is there any other way to stop it, other than face her?"

"Maybe," I said. "But I doubt it. Even if I can find her before she hurts someone else... I don't know. I just don't know. If I can get to her... I don't know, Amanda."

She nodded again, settled down in the seat and stared out through the windshield as the Camaro ate up the road, one tight bend after another. In different circumstances, I would have been enjoying the hell out of the ride. As it was, I don't even remember it. One thing I did know, however: this thing was all on me. Ronnie had been shot because of me. *Who the hell will it be next?* I wondered as I swung the car onto East Brow.

Yeah, it was on me; my fault, and I had to stop it.

When we got home, I went straight to the bedroom and reinserted the battery into my iPhone. Then I held it close to my lips.

"Are you listening? If you are, pin your damned ears back: I'm coming for you. I'm going to find you; I'm going to get you. If I have to kill you, I will. The stunt you just pulled? You didn't need to do that. You already had my attention…"

The iPhone buzzed in my hand, the screen lit up, *Amanda? What the hell?*

She was standing behind me, listening, her arms folded, her iPhone, still without its battery, lay on the bed.

"Who is it?" she asked.

I shook my head and answered the phone, "Who is this?"

"Hello, Harry," the voice was female, light, soft, sexy. "You know who it is. Yes, I was listening to you. I suppose you'll put a stop to that now. Oh well, it was fun while it lasted."

"Who the hell are you? What do you want?"

"My name… my name is Calaway Jones. What do I want? I want you, Harry. You've upset some really nasty people, and they want you gone, and they've hired me to make you leave."

The choice of words was intriguing. Not a death threat; nothing that could be used as evidence. I was stunned, not by what she said but by her casual attitude, her temerity, by the naked brass balls she had to call me. I was speechless.

"Cat got your tongue, Harry?"

"If it's me you want, why the hell are you screwing around with my wife and friends? I'm not hiding from you."

"True, but you should be. I'm good, Harry; very good. As to your friends… well, they're just a means to an end, to… hurt you without… hurting you, I suppose would be a good way to put it."

"What the hell are you talking about? If it's me you want, that's fine; just leave my wife and friends out of it."

"It is you, and I will get around to you, eventually. In the meantime…"

My blood was boiling. This was crazy. I was having a conversation with a contract killer out to terminate me, and she was treating the whole thing like it was some sort of fun game.

"You leave them out of this, damn you. You got a beef with me, bring it on, you crazy bitch. But you…"

"Oh come on, Harry. I'm not crazy. Far from it. What do you think I am, a barbarian? I do what I do for money, not just because I can. What the hell did you do to… to my employer to make him so angry?"

"I kicked his friggin' cat. What d'you think I did? I put him away for twenty-five years, federal; he'll do every minute of it if he doesn't die first."

"Is that it? Come on, Harry. There has to be more to it than that. This man is… is… well, he wants me to, 'hurt you more than you hurt him.' I think those were the words."

"You spoke to him?"

She laughed; it sounded like a gurgling mountain creek. Any other time it would have been entrancing. As it was…

"Nice try, Harry. No. I've never met him. Until I heard you say it, I didn't even know his name. No, it was Mr. Tree who told me that. He's a strange one, isn't he? He doesn't like you at all, Harry."

"You think I believe that? I don't. Call it off," I said. "Quit, while you can. If you don't…"

"If I don't, what? What will you do, Harry? You know nothing about me. You don't know where I am, or what I'm capable of. Your man— what's his name? Ronnie? He meant nothing to me. I had no need to kill him, nor even hurt him, well, not too much." She'd thrown caution to the wind. She was telling it like it was.

"I hurt him just enough to get your attention. I could just as easily have put two in the back of his neck instead of his ass. He was just a means to get to you. Amanda? Now she's different. Part of my contract is to deal with her *before* I get around to you—my employer wants you to know what it feels like to lose a loved one—and I always fulfill my contracts. Well, now you know, and I think I've said enough for tonight. Sleep well, Harry. Look after Amanda. She's lovely; you're a lucky man... or not. I'll talk to you again soon."

The phone went dead. I looked at the screen; nothing. I went to "recent calls." There were no calls listed newer than ten o'clock, before I first removed the battery. I removed it again and threw it down on the nightstand, then I sat down on the bed, next to Amanda, put my arm around her, and pulled her in close. *Damn Harper to hell. He has me by the shorts. If screwing with my head was his plan, it's working. He's really messing with my mind. Calaway Jones? Who the hell is this woman? Where did she come from? Benny... What the hell is he doing?*

I really needed to tell Amanda what the bitch on the phone had said, about her being a target, but I couldn't. I would have to tell Kate and Lonnie though.

Chapter 13
Friday, July 14, 10am

I called Bob early that Friday morning to tell him not to come to the house but to meet me at the office at ten, and that I'd bring Amanda with me. After the talk with... Calaway Jones or whoever she was the night before, I wasn't about to let her, Amanda, out of my sight.

We were there first, some thirty minutes early. I waited as the gate rolled open and then I drove the Camaro inside. I pulled into my space and, as I pushed the gear shift into the park position, I happened to glance sideways out of the passenger side window... just in time to see a black Mini Cooper drive slowly by. The windows were tinted so I couldn't see the driver, but I had a real good idea who it was. I almost slammed the car into gear and went after it, but the gate was already rolling shut and knew I'd never make it onto the street in time to catch her, if it was her. So I acted like nothing had happened, and we went inside.

The first thing I did, was check the security monitors. The Mini was there, but only for a second or two, and the camera angle was too high for me to get a good view of the windshield. Was it the same one I saw at the hospital? I didn't know, but I had a strong feeling that it was.

Slowly, over the next twenty minutes, the others arrived, Jacque first, then Bob and Kate together, then Lonnie; Tim was the last to arrive. He pushed backward through the door into the conference room, his arms and hands full—a plastic grocery bag with a box of Krispy Kreams inside clamped in his teeth, his laptop under one arm, a cardboard tray with eight Starbucks coffees in his hands, and his glasses precariously perched at the tip of his nose.

Carefully, he placed the cardboard tray on the table, took the bag from his teeth and set it down beside the coffee, then his laptop. Finally, he stood upright, shoved his glasses up the bridge of his nose with a forefinger, flung his arms in the air, his head back and stretched.

"I brought coffee and donuts," he said, stating the obvious. "My treat, yeah?" The grin was almost too much to bear.

We all looked up at him in wonder. As always, he was in the best of moods. The boy was not of this world; couldn't be.

"Thanks, Tim," I said, grabbing a coffee and handing it to Amanda and then taking one for myself.

I waited until everyone was seated and supplied with coffee and Krispy Kreams, then I opened my legal pad and wrote at the top, "Is it safe to talk freely in here?" Then I shoved the pad to where Tim could see it.

He shrugged, shook his head, got to his feet, and left the room. He was back a few minutes later with a FedEx package. He opened it. Inside was a second, smaller box that contained an instrument that looked a lot like an early model cell phone. He inserted the batteries that came with it, turned it on, fiddled with it for a minute, then took out his burner phone, turned it on, looked at it, and nodded.

"Okay," he said, grinning at everyone. "All clear. We can talk freely now. This is a Titan jamming device. It jams everything—all cell frequencies: 4g, 3g, WiFi, GPS trackers. You name it. After our talk yesterday, Mr. Starke, I took the liberty of ordering one. Under the circs, I didn't think you'd mind." He shrugged, leaned back in his seat, dipped his donut in his coffee, and nibbled on it.

I opened my iPad…

"Ummm," Tim said. "You can't get online. No WiFi, remember?"

I looked at him and shook my head. He grinned back at me and shoved his glasses up the bridge of his nose.

"Tim," I said. "Why the hell don't you get those things fixed so that they don't keep sliding off your nose?"

"I really should, shouldn't I," he said, poking at them yet again. "One of these days, yeah?"

I gazed around the table. Everyone was looking at me expectantly. I sighed, laced my fingers together behind my neck, leaned back in my chair, and stared up at the ceiling. I didn't know where the hell to begin. I had Amanda seated right next to me and I sure as hell didn't want her to learn that she was just as much a target as I was, but I couldn't see a way around it. One way or another...

I leaned forward, folded my arms on the edge of the table, and said, "She called me last night."

There was an audible gasp from Jacque; the rest of the group just stared at me, waiting for me to go on. I did.

"It was short, maybe three minutes, no more. She told me her name is Calaway Jones. Maybe it is; maybe it isn't, but whoever she is, she's supremely confident and a pro, very much a pro. I could tell that from her attitude. The hit on Ronnie, the shot at Amanda, the smiley faces, were all aimed directly at me, to get my attention—so she said—but more, I think to intimidate me, to mess with my head. You guys are not her target; that's me." I made no mention of Amanda.

"She said that she'd never spoken to the person who hired her, but that she'd done all of her business with Lester Tree."

"So it is Harper?" Kate asked.

"Oh yes. She didn't actually admit it; not directly. She said she didn't even know his name until she heard it from me—yes, Tim, she was listening in through the phones as you thought. So now the question becomes: how the hell do we stop her?"

"You know how," Bob said, rocking on the back legs of his chair. "I told you that yesterday. You cut the head off the snake, in this case, Harper. You put Harper out of the picture, and the contract becomes null and void."

"Perhaps," I said. "But right now, that's not the answer I'm looking for. I need to find this Calaway Jones…"

"Oh for Christ's sake, Harry," Bob said, as the front legs of his chair hit the floor with a crack. "That's not going to get it. Harper's a damned terrier. You hide one bone, he'll dig around 'til he finds another. We have to stop this mess at the source, and the source is him. Get with the friggin' program, Harry."

I looked at Kate. She shrugged, but she was shaking her head. What Bob was proposing was murder. The thing was, I knew he was right; Harper would never give up until one of us—him or me—was dead. We could trap him, get him for conspiracy to commit murder; he'd get another twenty years for that, but it wouldn't stop him. Nothing would.

"Bob's right," Lonnie said. "Harper's got to go. He says he can get it done. If so, let him. If he can't, I can. One call is all it would take."

I heaved a sigh and shook my head.

"Damn it," Bob said as he slammed his clenched fists down on the table. "You know what? It's not your damned call, Harry. What if this bitch kills Amanda, or me, or Kate? It will be on your head. Is that what you want?"

He knew I didn't, and I knew he was right, but I still couldn't condone murder.

"I'll handle it, Bob," I said, quietly. "Leave it to me, okay."

"Yeah, yeah, that's what I'll do. I'll leave it to *you*," the sarcasm was heavy in his voice.

"Enough!" I snapped at him. "I have enough to deal with without having to worry about you. I need you to help me, not hinder me. You on board, or not?"

He sat back in his chair, folded his arms and said, almost under his breath, "You know I am."

"Lonnie? Kate?"

They both nodded.

"Okay, good. This is what I want: The office is closed until further notice. I want Amanda, Jacque, Tim, Ronnie, when he gets out of the hospital, to stay locked down tight until I can find this woman. If I need you, I'll get hold of you. Stay off your smart phones; use the burners Tim gave you. Tim, what's the range of this thing?" I picked up the Titan.

"Seventy-five, maybe a hundred feet."

"Okay. It stays on, all the time."

"Nope," Tim said. "If it stays on, we have no WiFi. You want to run the Web on your devices, it has to be turned off. The computers are okay. I use a dedicated connection for those."

"I knew that," I said, and I did. I just wasn't thinking. "So we just turn it on when we need to talk then?"

Tim nodded.

"That's it then. I need to make a call. How do I turn this thing off?"

Tim took it from me and turned it off. No sooner had he done so than my own burner phone rang.

I looked around the table. They were all watching me. I shrugged and answered it.

"Harry it's me. Why the hell don't you answer your damn phone. I've been trying to reach you for…"

"Benny!" I looked at Bob. He smiled.

"I hope to hell you have good news for me."

"North Chamberlain, Harry, and you'd better get the lead out. He's loading crap into his car. Looks like he's about to run."

He gave me the address, and I jumped to my feet.

"Bob, you're with me, now! Kate, I need you to look after Amanda. I'll explain later."

"Explain what?" Amanda asked, looking worried.

"Later, Sweetie. I, we, gotta go. Shady's about to make a run for it. The rest of you... Lonnie?" I looked at him, my eyebrows raised.

"Yeah, go on get outa here."

And we did.

Chapter 14
Friday, July 14, 11:30am

On any normal day, in any normal car, it would have been a good ten-minute drive to the address that Benny had given me, more in heavy traffic. This, however, was neither a normal day or car, and the traffic was relatively light, thank God.

I gunned the Camaro north on Georgia, made a right on Fifth, a left on Houston, a right on Fourth, ran the red light at McKenzie Arena and hurtled down onto Riverfront Parkway. From there it was almost a straight run to Wilcox; the HUD went over ninety several times as I sped by vehicle after vehicle. Fortunately, the lights at Wilcox were green, and there was no hold up there. I made a fast right over the railway yards, down the hill to Holtzclaw and damn me if the light wasn't against me there. I waited, but only for a second or so, and then gunned the Camaro through a gap in the traffic and on toward Chamberlain where I made a left. I made that drive in only five minutes, and you know what? I do believe I could have done it quicker.

"Geez, Harry. Where the hell d'you learn to drive like that?" Bob asked as he let loose of the strap.

"At the Academy. Where else? Look, there's Benny's pickup."

As I pulled up behind him, he stuck his arm out of the window, waved and pointed at the house across the street, and then, with a squeal of tires, he was away, gone.

The trunk of the late model, dark metallic blue BMW M6 parked on the driveway was open. We were in time.

"Let's go," I said.

I got out of the car and ran across the road, into the driveway, and went to the side of the house; Bob followed less than a second behind me.

I pulled the VP9, nodded, and pointed toward the back of the house, my eyebrows raised. He nodded back and ran around the side toward the rear; I went around the front and in through the front door.

"Going somewhere, Shady?" I asked, pleasantly.

If I told you that I took Shady by surprise, that would be the understatement of the year. He was so shocked he dropped the cardboard box he was carrying; it hit the floor and burst wide open, spilling at least a dozen pairs of fancy shoes all over the floor.

For a moment, he stood stock still, frozen. Then, like a scalded cat, he spun round and ran through the house. He flung open the back door and ran out, straight into Bob's arms.

Now you have to understand that Bob's a big guy, a very tough character. He's about as tall as I am—six-two—but he weighs two-sixty; that's forty-five pounds heavier than me. Shady, on the other hand, weighed in at around one-eighty-five. It was no contest.

"Hey, Shady," he said, grinning. "Hold on, old son. What's the hurry?"

He fought like the aforementioned scalded cat, kicking and biting and struggling, but Bob simply put the squeeze on him and slowly Shady's struggles weakened.

"You gonna calm down, or do I have to break something?" Bob asked, reasonably, as he bodily carried him back into the living room.

I watched, smiling, as the air slowly leaked out of the smaller man and with it any further resistance.

"Lemme go, you fat pig. Pu' me down. Get away from me. I ain' forgot what you done to m'man Henry."

He was referring to an incident almost a year ago when Bob... Well, that's a story for another day; let's just say that Henry Gold didn't survive the encounter. But "fat"? Hah, Bob's anything but.

"Calm down, Shady," I said, dragging a chair out from the table. "Talking about Henry. Where's Duvon? I expected to find him here too." Duvon

James was Henry Gold's partner until… well, as I said, that's another story.

"He ain't here," Tree gasped. "Gone to Florida, an' that's where I'm goin' too."

I nodded and shoved the chair toward him. "Here sit down. We just want to talk to you; ask you a few questions. Behave yourself and… Well, you can be on your way to wherever the hell you like. You up for that?"

"Yeah, yeah, just get this friggin' bear offa me."

I nodded, and Bob lowered him to his feet, grabbed his shoulders, spun him around, and forced him down onto the chair.

"Sit still, Shady," he growled. "Make one sudden move, and you'll get what Henry got."

Shady actually shuddered, but he did as he was told and sat rigidly upright.

He was a tall man, maybe six feet, slim, light skinned with well-cared for dreadlocks, and he liked to dress well: a blue and white Nike golf shirt, dark blue golf pants and pale blue, denim fabric Italian shoes. No, Shady was no gang banger; far from it.

"What the hell d'you want, Starke? I ain't… Ow, ow, ow. Whadda hell? Wha' fo you do dat?" He howled, rubbing the back of his skull.

Bob had pulled one his forty-fives and tapped him on the back of the head.

"Okay, Bob," I said, pulling up another chair and setting it down in front of Shady. "I'll take it from here."

"Take what? Whachoo talkin' about, Starke?"

I had to smile at that. He sounded just like Gary Coleman in Diff'rent Strokes.

I took the small digital recorder from my jacket pocket, turned it on and set it on the table just to Shady's left—Bob was standing behind him, holding his arms. I sat down on the chair in front of him, really close; my knees almost touching his.

"Okay, Shady," I said. "Let's talk, but first... Well, there are two ways we can do this; both affect your wellbeing. We can do it the easy way or... the *painful* way: your choice. What's it to be?"

"Screw you, Starke. I ain't tellin' you nothin'. I don't know nothin'."

I nodded, "Painful it is, then," I said, pulling the VP9 from its holster under my arm.

"Whoa!" He reared back on his chair, almost tipping it over backward, but Bob caught him and set him upright again.

"What you doin', man? I told yuh, I don't know nothin'."

I leaned forward, my elbows on my knees the barrel of the VP9 angled upward toward his nose.

"You sure you don't want to reconsider, Shady?"

145

"I done told yuh…" I reached out and tapped him gently on the bridge of his nose with the VP9. It's kind of heavy for a nine mil, and it had quite an effect on poor Shady.

"Agh. Ow, ow. Oh shit. Oh, oh. You broke my nose. Ow, ow."

He tore his arm loose from Bob's grasp and cradled it. I hadn't hurt him. Well, only a little. It would bruise, but I hadn't broken the skin. The nose; it's so sensitive, though, you know?

"Ready to talk, Shady?"

"Talk about what?" he yelled. No Ebonics now. "What the hell do you want, Starke?"

"When did you last talk to Little Billy Harper?"

"I ain't…" Bob grabbed his arms and pulled them back; I tapped him again.

"*Owuh*. Oh shit. I'm telling you, Harry…"

I raised the VP9 again. "Nooo, for Christ's sake don't do that again. Look, I ain't heard from Harper in more'n a month, okay? Please! Don't do that shit again."

I leaned back in my chair and stared at him, slapping the palm of my left hand with the barrel of the gun. He watched, mesmerized. His damn head was nodding in time with my hand.

"You talked to him more than a month ago?"

He nodded, vigorously.

"On the phone, or in person?"

146

"In person; in person. He as't me to go to the prison, so I did."

"So tell me," I said. "A month ago; at the prison; in Atlanta. What did you two talk about?" I continued slowly slapping the palm of my hand.

"Noth... *Whoa. Stop.*"

I relaxed, leaned back again, and continued the hypnotic slapping.

"We... we talked about you, some. He don't like you worth a damn, Harry."

"What did he say about me, Shady?"

"Just that. No, no. Honest. That was it."

"So," I said, easily, "you went all the way to Atlanta just so that he could tell you that he doesn't like me; that right?"

He stared at me uneasily, "Well, no. Not exactly."

"So what, *exactly*?"

"He needed some toiletries, an' stuff. I took 'em to him."

My arm uncoiled liked a striking cobra, *SLAP!* I hammered the flat of the barrel of the VP9 down hard on his kneecap.

"*Eeeeek!*" he yelled. He would have come up out of the chair if Bob hadn't been holding him down. *"Oh God. Oh hell. You sadistic son of a bitch."*

For what must have been at least a minute, he sat there, breathing hard, moaning, rubbing his knee. I hadn't damaged it. Oh, it was probably bruised, but I hadn't broken anything. I knew what I was doing.

"I'll ask you just one more time, Shady. What did you two talk about?"

"I... can't, Harry, for God's sake. He'll have me killed. *He will!* You know what he's like. He's one crazy bastard." He began to shudder uncontrollably.

"Calm down, Shady. I'm not going to hurt you."

"You already did, you sick son of a bitch. Oh my God."

"He may not hurt you," Bob said, coming around the front, the Sig forty-five in his hand. "But I will. Get up, Harry. Let me have a go at him."

Shady was shaking his head, "No, man. No!"

I got up; Bob sat down. Shady whimpered with fear.

"Now," Bob said. "Spill it; all of it."

Shady just sat there, his face white as a ghost, even his teeth were chattering, but still he shook his head. *Geez, he really is scared of Little Billy.*

Bob nodded, thumbed back the hammer, placed the muzzle of his gun against Shady's left knee and... pulled the trigger. There was a loud click as the hammer hit the firing pin, followed by the most ungodly howl from Shady, and then he slumped down in the chair. For a moment, I thought he'd passed out, but he hadn't. He looked up at me like a wounded puppy and mouthed, "Please, Harry?"

I almost felt sorry for him, but then I remembered my brother Henry and how he had died at the hands of Duvon James, one of Lester Tree's mobsters, and I nodded at Bob.

He racked a round into the chamber of the 1911—that action re-cocked the hammer—then he gently placed the muzzle of the gun against Shady's right knee cap, the one I had smacked with the VP9. Shady stared at the gun, mesmerized, unable to speak.

I put a restraining hand on Bob's shoulder, "No Bob, that wouldn't just cripple him, it would blow his damned leg off. Here, use this."

I reached down for my ankle piece and handed it to him, a small, Glock 26 subcompact semi-automatic. "There's one in the chamber." There was, too, and I was kind of leery that Bob would actually do it.

"Last chance, Shady," Bob said. "You gonna talk?"

He was shaking from head to toe, but he nodded and said, breathlessly, "What do you want to know?"

"Let me sit down, Bob," I said. He rose to his feet, handed the Glock to me, and I sat.

"Now, I want to know about the contract he put out on me."

"I don't know…" I lifted the Glock.

"*Stop*!" he yelled. "I'm telling you what I know, okay? I was just gonna tell you that I don't know the details of the contract, just… well, just that… that he paid her a bunch of money, I do know that: $250k. Half up front; the rest when the job is done."

"Her? Who's this *her*?"

"It's a woman… He told me to contact her an' give her an envelope. I didn't open it. I don't know what was in it. I don't know anything."

"He's lying through his damned teeth," Bob said, taking a step forward. "Let me have another go at him."

"*No, no*. I ain't. I swear I don't know nothin'."

"Look at me, Shady," I said. He didn't.

"I said *look at me!*" I slammed the Glock down on his knee; on the same spot I'd hit before.

"*Aaargh!*" He howled like a cat in heat.

"One more time, Shady. Look at me."

He did. He looked me in the eye.

"Now, tell me again. Who is she? I'll know if you're lying, and…"

He looked away, "I told you. I don't know." He was lying. He couldn't look me in the eye.

I raised the Glock and placed the muzzle against his kneecap, "If I pull the trigger, Shady," I said, quietly, "you've been around. You know what kind of damage a contact wound can do. You'll never walk again. Now, I'm going to count to three, and then I'm going to blow your goddamn kneecap to hell and back. One... Two..." I took a deep breath, sat a little more upright on my chair, pressed the muzzle into his flesh a little harder, and...

"Okayokayokay *okay,*" he gasped.

I let out my breath and relaxed, removed the Glock from his knee and leaned back in my seat. *Jesus, that was close!*

"Go on," I said.

"Shit, shit, *shit*... Her name is Calaway Jones. She's an Israeli. An assassin. He hired her to kill you." *So that really is her name.*

"And that's it? Look at me, Shady. I said, is that it?"

His face didn't move, but his eyes did. He was about to lie again.

"Don't do it, Shady. Don't lie to me." I banged the muzzle of the Glock hard against his knee. He screwed up his eyes in pain; yeah, that knee was going to bruise, and it was going to be painful for a while.

"I know you, Shady. You can't help yourself. You looked in the envelope. Didn't you? What was in it? Tell me everything."

"I... I..." He hung his head. "I can't, Harry. They'll kill me. Please... give me a break."

"A break? A friggin' break? I'm giving you a whole lot more of a break than you deserve, more than you gave my brother. You remember my brother, don't you, Shady?"

He looked up at me, his eyes wide.

"You're lucky I *don't* blow your damned head off, let alone your knee. Now spill it. Before I lose patience with you."

"Okay... okay. I did glance through it. Billy hired her to kill you, but it was more than that. He wanted you to suffer, suffer real bad. She's supposed to screw with your head. Maybe kill or hurt some of your people... or... family before she kills you. Look, Harry. I had nothing to do with it. My job was just to find her and give her the envelope is all, and that's what I did. When you got here, I was just about to head out to West Palm. I'm done with this mess and Harper. He's crazy. I mean it. He's lost it, Harry. I'm done with 'im, and with Chattanooga. I'll be glad if I never see this damned city again. I swear."

"So you found her. Where?"

"In Paris. Wasn't easy. I had to go to the dark web, find someone who knew her. She's a contractor, a mercenary, she advertises, for Christ's sake."

"And?"

"And I contacted her. That's it."

"No, Shady. That wasn't it. People in her line of business are very careful. They don't just drop everything and run right on over. What did you tell her?"

"I didn't have to tell her anything. She already knew him, Little Billy. She's done work for him before. All I did was tell her he had a job for her and what the pay was. She told me to meet her in Atlanta, at Starbucks on West Paces Ferry Road, and I did."

"What flight was she on?"

"Hell, I don't know. She got into Atlanta around two o'clock in the afternoon on June 30. I didn't go to the airport. I met her as arranged, after three-thirty at Starbucks, an' I give her the envelope, and that's it, Harry; I swear."

"How did you contact her? Phone? Email? What?"

"Phone. Throwaway."

"And now?"

There was that evasive look again, "Shady…"

"Yeah, I have a number, but she'll…"

"You won't get out of this house if you don't, now give."

He did, and I made a note of it.

"Give me your number, Shady."

He did, and I made a note of that.

"One more thing," I said. "Did you see what she was driving?"

"No... no, Harry; I swear it. I was in Starbucks seated at a table, and she just walked in. She must have parked somewhere out of sight, an' she made me leave first."

"Okay, so how the hell did you know how to recognize her? Tell me about her."

"She told me she'd be wearing a pale blue shirt and black jeans. She came in; I waved at her. That's it."

"Describe her. What did she look like?"

"I dunno. She was hot...ish. Medium build. Looked to be about twenny-five or six, five-eight or nine, short brown hair, no tits, pretty face... but not... Hell, now I think about it, she was quite ordinary."

"You're sure you didn't see her car?"

"I didn't. I swear I didn't. I handed her the bag, she looked inside, and then left. That was it. C'mon, Harry. Can I go now?"

"Bag?" I asked. "What bag?"

Again, he tried to avoid my eyes, but a twitch of the Glock got his attention.

"She'd asked me to get a few things for her... you know..."

"Shady, you're really beginning to get on my nerves. What things?"

"A subcompact Beretta nine mill with suppressor; an' a twen'y-two Beretta 71, an' a suppressor for that too, and... an' a... Sig M400 with a folding stock, a scope and a suppressor... and 200 rounds for each."

Inwardly, I heaved a sigh. I'd feared the worst, and that's what I now knew I was facing. The Beretta 71 was a Mossad favorite. It was a "close up and personal" weapon, and it must have been what she'd used to shoot Ronnie. The M400 was a top-of-the-line AR-15. It, coupled with a good scope, and in the right hands, was... I shook my head and looked at Bob. He shrugged.

"What else are you not telling me?" I asked.

"That's all of it, Harry. I swear."

"Did she make arrangements to call you, or for you to call her?"

He shook his head. "No. She took my number and said if she needed anything, she'd call. So far, she hasn't."

"Okay," I said, leaning back in my seat. "Here's where we stand. You can go, but keep your phone handy. *Do not get rid of it.* You *do not* tell Harper or this Jones woman that we've had this conversation. You understand?"

He nodded. I stared at him. He squirmed uncomfortably.

"If you hear from her, or Harper, you call me," I gave him the number of the burner phone I was using. "And you do it immediately. If I find out that you've spoken to either of them and not told me, I'll hunt you down. Got it?"

He nodded, vigorously.

"Shady," I said, as I slid the Glock into its holster, "this is the only warning you'll ever get from me. Get out of town, now, today, and stay out. You stay the hell away from me and mine. You come back, you'd better be ready to kill me because if you don't, I won't kill you, I'll put you in a wheelchair for the rest of your life. You hear me?"

"Yeah, yeah... *yeah!* I hear yuh." He started to get up.

"Look at me, Shady." He did. "I mean it."

He nodded, grabbed his cardboard box, gathered up the scattered shoes, shoved them inside, and all but ran out of the front door, leaving Bob and me sitting there watching him go.

We heard the BMW roar to life, and the gravel fly as he reversed out onto North Chamberlain, and then the squeal of tires as he headed north toward Bonnie Oaks. I picked up the recorder and turned it off.

"Hey," Bob said, as walked across the street to the Camaro. "Are you gonna let me drive this beast or not?"

"Not!" I said, grinning sideways at him.

"Hah, some pal you are."

"By the way," I said, "How come you didn't have one in the pipe when you frightened the crap out of him? That's not like you."

"I cleared it when I was round back of the house before we went in. Thought it might be useful; it was. The twin, though…" He patted the grip under his right arm. "Always… Hey, that Glock of yours *was* ready to go. Would you really have done it?"

"Done what?"

"You know what. Blow his damned kneecap off?"

Again, I grinned at him, but I said nothing. Hell, I didn't know the answer to that one myself but… Probably not.

Chapter 15
Friday, July 14, Early Afternoon

From Chamberlain, it was less than a couple of miles to Erlanger hospital and only a block out of my way on the drive back to the office, so I called to find out if I could pick up Ronnie. I couldn't. He'd somehow gotten a staph infection, and they wanted to keep an eye on him for a few days so it was a little after midday when Bob and I arrived back at my office.

The parking lot was empty, except for Tim's Honda, so I assumed he was still there, which was what I expected. I'd asked him to wait until we got back. And he had; he was back in his lair, in front of the array of flat screen monitors that were his world. He was staring up at one of them as he typed, his fingers almost a blur, but he looked up and smiled when I walked in—Bob was making coffee.

"Is that thing on?" I asked, nodding at the Titan jamming device on his desk.

He shook his head, and flipped the switch, "It is now."

He grinned up at me, took off his glasses, wiped them on the tail of his untucked shirt, put them back on and shoved them up the bridge of his nose.

"Where is everybody?" I asked.

"Amanda took them all to lunch. They're at the Flatiron if you want to go join them."

I shook my head, "Nope, I'll send Bob. I need you to track someone down for me. Did they say when they were coming back?"

"Not long, I suppose, but they left only about ten minutes ago.

I nodded.

"I'll have to turn that thing off again if you want to use your laptop," he was referring to the Titan device. "I told you: nothing in here works when it's on, except for my computers, which are hardwired. Phones, tablets, WiFi, listening devices, nada." He reached for the switch.

"Whoa. No, don't turn it off. I need to talk to Bob first, and then I need to explain what we're looking for. Just hold everything for a minute. I'll be right back."

I went looking for Bob. I found him making coffee for two, one of which I hoped was for me.

"Sorry, Buddy," I said, taking one of the mugs from the countertop. "I need you to go to the Flatiron. They're all there, eating lunch. Knowing what we now know, I wish to hell they hadn't gone. Go get 'em back, okay? Keep an eye out for her, this Calaway Jones. She could be lurking anywhere. Make sure they don't have any smartphones with 'em. Do... oh hell, Bob. You know what to do. I don't need to tell you."

"No, Harry. You don't. Kate and Lonnie are there, so no problem…"

"You don't know that. They don't know what we're up against, and please don't tell them. Let me do that when they get here. I don't want Amanda to know that she's a target."

"You got it. I'll be back!"

I screwed up my eyes, "*Schwarzenegger?*"

"Yeah, him. Good, eh?" He asked as he opened the side door. "Hasta La Vista, Baby."

I don't think I'd heard anything quite so stupid come out of his mouth since I'd known him. It was the *worst* impression, *ever*. I shook my head, dropped a splash of half-and-half into my coffee— something I rarely ever did, but what the hell?— and went back to talk to Tim.

"Okay, Tim. Is that thing still on?"

"Yup, 'till you tell me different."

"Right. You might want to take notes. So we're looking for an ex-Mossad agent named Calaway Jones." He made a note of it on his iPad.

"Lester Tree said he found her on the dark web, advertising as a mercenary. She's living in Paris. Billy Harper has hired her…"

"Oh my," he looked up at me, concern written all over his face. "For what?"

"Never mind that, for now. Just concentrate on tracking her down. She flew into Atlanta from Paris around two o'clock in the afternoon on June

30. She met with Shady at a Starbucks on West Paces Ferry Road in Atlanta." I handed him my recorder. "Here, you can listen to her description. Don't play it with the jammer off."

He nodded.

"Okay, do your thing."

"The Dark Web, huh?"

He turned to his keyboard, and for several minutes he tapped, stopping now and then to read the screens.

"Here we go." He leaned back in his chair. "Not sure, but I think this might be it."

On the screen in front of him was a... an advertisement, I suppose you could call it. All it was, was a single line of text—no photograph. No name—that read:

"Cleaner for hire. CJ." and there was a Paris phone number.

I looked at him, "You think?"

He shrugged. The glasses fell off the end of his nose onto the keyboard.

"Turn that thing off. I'll call the number."

It rang twice and then went to voicemail: it was cryptic, three words only, "Leave a message." The voice was electronically distorted. I couldn't tell if it was male or female, nor did I care.

I didn't leave a message. Instead, I hit the switch and turned Tim's fancy piece of hardware back on.

"Any chance you could trace it?"

He shook his head, "Possibly. It wouldn't do you any good, though. If she's as smart as we think she is…"

I nodded, "Let's see if we can find her. How about flights from Paris on June 30?" I asked.

He tapped, paused, tapped some more, repeated the process, then said, "Here we are. Flight number 8504 from Paris arrived Atlanta at one-fifty in the afternoon of June 30. Sounds about right."

He was right. It did.

"Can you get into the passenger manifest?"

"I can, but good luck on that one. There's no way she'd be traveling under the name Calaway Jones, but let's take a look."

He tapped some more.

"There were two hundred twenty-seven people on the flight, including passengers and crew. One hundred and thirty-six of them were French nationals. Of those, only eleven were women traveling alone. Let's see who they were. Hmmm… hmmm… Nope. Only five of them come even close to a match: Marie Rousseau, Marcie Deneuve, Genevieve Charon, Renée Fournier, and Sylvie Roux."

"Passport photos?"

"Of course, but I can't access them... well, not quickly."

"Okay. What about the airport security cameras?"

"Oh yeah. I can do that. It's simple enough. Most CCT systems are still using software that's more than ten years old. Give me a couple of minutes."

Less than a minute later we were looking at a mosaic of images on three different screens, all inside Hartsfield International Airport, all time stamped and labeled Concourse A, and was it ever crowded. More tapping. The screens were a blur, changing every second. Then:

"Here we go... Terminal One... Gate... Gotcha. Now... June... 30 at... one-forty-five... Yes!"

"How the hell do you do that, Tim?"

He grinned up at me, flipped his glasses with his forefinger, and said, "I could tell ya, but..."

"Yeah, yeah, that's what I pay you for, right. So, the flight hadn't yet arrived at this point?"

"No, not yet."

I watched as the time stamp ticked away the seconds at the bottom of the screen. Just a few more minutes. *Nope! Need to go faster.*

"Fast forward it, Tim. Let's see the passengers." He did.

The camera must have been positioned by an expert. The angle of view was perfect, inclined slightly downward toward the gate exit doors.

We watched as the passengers streamed out into the concourse. I had him pause the feed and take a screenshot every now and then when a likely female individual appeared; there were a bunch of them. Some we were able to eliminate immediately because they were obviously traveling with someone. We knew there were supposed to be five women of interest flying alone, and those we thought we'd identified, not by name, but by general appearance. One, we were able to eliminate immediately. She was short, blonde and overweight; the blonde hair could be a wig; the extra weight could be padding, but the height... no, not possible. That left us with four likely candidates.

I had Tim rerun the footage of each one. I was looking for something in their demeanor or appearance that might give her away."

"Hey. What's going on?"

I turned around. It was Amanda.

"We're just checking some airport security footage. Where are the others?"

"They're here. In the outer office. Do you want to see anyone in particular, other than me, of course?" she asked, smiling.

"You for sure; the others, yeah, but in the conference room in ten or fifteen minutes."

She nodded, stared at the screens, then at Tim, then at me, then she shrugged and, with a swish of her skirt, she turned and went back out to join the rest of the group.

"Okay," I said, turning back to Tim. "Run it again."

He did, and again, and several more times. I was able to tentatively eliminate two more. They both looked as if they didn't have a care in the world. I figured a woman on a mission would be a little more serious... resolute? Eh, staid might be a better word, and two of them were. Even so, I had Tim take close-up screenshots of all four faces, which he did.

One, however, stood out. Not because of anything other than that she managed to keep her face hidden, no not covered, nor was it an obvious attempt to avoid the camera. It was just a slight angling of the head downward and to one side, and it worked. It wasn't anything anyone would ordinarily pick up on, but I was looking for it. If it was intentional, this woman was good, highly-trained, and that too fit the bill. *Hmmm. I wonder. Could be... Could be... Could... be!*

She had one of those carry-on suitcases, a rollaway, with wheels and a handle. She was about the right height—given that she was wearing heels. But she had long—way past her shoulders—

thick, auburn hair that covered her ears and most of the left side of her face, well-developed breasts... *But Shady said she was flat chested. Padding... and a wig. That's her!*

"Stop," I said, "That's her, Tim."

"You think?"

She was wearing a blue skirt and a white top. Shady said she was wearing black jeans and blue top. *She must have changed clothes and gotten rid of the wig and breast pads. Yeah, she's a pro. No doubt about it.*

"Yup. I do. We need a clear shot of her face. Can you do that?"

"Let's... see... hmmm..."

The images flickered and turned as he flipped from one camera to the next. It wasn't a quick or easy process, but somehow, he was able to follow her along the length of the concourse to the elevators where he lost her. She walked with a purpose, bolt upright, perfect posture, but always with her head angled so that it was just a little out of line for any of the cameras to get a good image of her face. What we ended up with was a half-dozen close-up photos of her head all taken at different angles. Tim assured me he could build a recognizable image of her. I doubted that very much, but what the hell did I know? He'd surprised me many times before. It would take time, so he said, but he could do it.

In the meantime, I had him record several pieces of footage of the woman and put them on a DVD.

"Now, what can you find out about this woman, this Calaway Jones?" I asked him.

"Dunno, but I'll do some searches, see what I come up with. If she's what you say she is, Mossad, there won't be a lot to find. I'll do my best. It might take me a while, though."

I nodded, "Give it your best shot, then come join us in the conference room; don't turn that machine off... It covers the entire suite of offices, right?" I tapped the Titan.

"Yeah, and then some. I would imagine our neighbors are getting really pissed off."

I shrugged and left him to it, grabbed a fresh mug of Dark Italian Roast and went to join the others.

"Hey, Guys," I said, dropping into my seat at the head of the table. "We think we have a lock on the contractor. She said her name is Calaway Jones. Our conversation with Lester Tree confirms that. I have Tim doing a search for her. In the meantime, you can take a look at this."

I slipped the DVD into the drive on my laptop, hit play and turned it so they could see the screen.

"This footage was taken on the International concourse at Hartsfield."

"Damn," Lonnie said. "She's hot… at least I think she is. Can't see her face…"

"And right there, you have it," I interrupted him. "How many of us could pull that off, walk the entire length of the concourse, almost a quarter-mile, without even once showing our face to the camera? She's good, *really good*."

"Is that all we have of her?" Kate asked.

"For now, yes. Tim says he may be able to build a composite of her face from a bunch of stills, but I don't know. Shady gave us her description, and it doesn't fit this woman too well, but I think the differences are cosmetic; it could be her…" I stared at the screen, "and I think it is."

I looked at them each in turn. No one said a word.

"Tree said," I continued, "she had no… that she was flat chested, and that she had short brown hair. That doesn't fit this woman, but the hair looks like it could be a wig, and she could be wearing a padded bra, right?"

Kate and Jacque nodded. Amanda stared at the screen, mesmerized, her face white, her hands clasped together in her lap. *Not good!*

"She's the right height," I continued. "She's confident and obviously in great physical shape. Yep, this, I think, is who we're looking for…"

"Maybe they're real," Kate said, thoughtfully. "She could have had her chest taped when she met with Tree."

The door opened and Tim entered, loaded like a damn Christmas tree with an open laptop in the crook of his right arm, his iPad under his other arm, a stylus between his teeth, and a large mug of coffee in his left hand. He sat down at the far end of the table, laid down his bits and pieces, did his thing with his glasses, and beamed down the length of the table at me. I suddenly realized who he reminded me of: that crazy movie critic you sometimes see on Fox News... Kevin McCarthy. *I love that guy.*

"You look pleased with yourself," I said.

"Not really. I don't have an image for you, yet, but I just ran some very deep searches for this Calaway Jones character."

"Okay. What did you find?"

He leaned forward, adjusted the screen of his laptop, did a couple of taps, then said, "Not much. She keeps a very low profile. From what little I could find around the Web, it seems she joined the Israeli army at the age of eighteen and was recruited into the IDF—the Israeli Defense Force—a year later, and into the Mossad a year after that as a member of Kidon—very nasty. Kidon is a very secretive division of the Mossad, which means she's quite special, Harry, because its members are *the elite* of the Mossad. They are

169

all expert assassins. They carry out black ops all over the world, including here in the U.S. Anyway, there she stayed until finally, in 2011, she went freelance. That makes her... what? Thirty-four, thirty-five?"

He looked up at me. I nodded. That also fit the profile of the woman at the airport.

"Go on."

"Not much has been heard of her since she went freelance. There are no photographs and... I strongly suspect that Calaway Jones is not her real name, but I could be wrong about that. Still, I could find no reference to a Calaway Jones either in the Israeli Army or IDF records, which means she must have been recruited under another name. Those records, if they ever existed, have been wiped. The name appeared only after she left the Mossad... Harry?" He stared up at me. "If what I've found is true, she's done some really bad stuff. She's thought to be responsible for the Karkov hit, along with several other high-profile international hits."

Yevgeny Karkov had been the Russian ambassador to London. He died a couple of years ago in a London hospital—some kind of poison. There were rumors at the time that he was planning to make a run for the Russian Presidency.

I stood and stared down at the image of the woman walking the concourse, looking at her, but not really seeing her. My mind was elsewhere. *She's a ghost. Calaway Jones is a ghost.*

"Hey!" Bob said, "Earth to Harry. Where the hell are you?"

I shrugged, "I was just thinking; if this woman is all Tim just said she is, we have our hands full."

I sat down again. The silence was, as they say, deafening.

Chapter 16
Friday, July 14, Late Afternoon

"So," Kate said. "We need a plan. Any ideas?" She was looking at me. I had none, and neither did anyone else.

For the next hour we talked, and we talked, and by five o'clock that afternoon we'd made little progress... well, I had, but it wasn't yet something I wanted to discuss, especially in front of Amanda. I had it in my head that I should offer Calaway Jones my head on a platter. What I mean by that is that maybe I should be the bait that would hook the fish. How I'd do that, I had yet to figure out.

At first, it was just the hair of an idea, but the more I thought about it, the more I convinced myself that it was the right thing to do, the only thing to do. I didn't want anyone else to get hurt— I already had Ronnie in the hospital, and I had a deep-seated feeling that if I allowed them to, things could only get worse.

Bob leaned back in his chair, laced his hands behind his neck, and stared at me. Jacque folded her arms and stared down at the table. Tim, at the far end of the table, leaned his elbows on the table and his chin in hands, and he stared at me; he looked like a skinny barn owl. Kate cradled her now cold cup of coffee in both hands and... yeah, she stared at me too. Lonnie just sat and stared at the now still image of the woman on the screen of the laptop. Amanda squeezed my hand under the table but said nothing. And they all waited for me to say something.

I thought about it, but nothing would come, only that sooner or later a face-to-face confrontation between me and what probably was the most dangerous opponent I'd ever encountered was… inevitable, and if I said the thought didn't bother me, I'd be lying.

During my years in the PD, and even those as a PI, I'd run into some pretty hairy characters—Sal De Luca being only the latest—and somehow, I'd always managed to come out on top. This time, though. Well, I just didn't know. If Calaway Jones was indeed a Mossad assassin, I'd need to be very careful, very careful indeed.

Finally, I inwardly heaved a sigh and said, "We have to go on the offensive. We can't let her take control of the battlefield. The first thing we have to do is find her, then we have to flush her out. Any thoughts… anyone?"

"Yeah," Bob said, his voice a low growl. "I have one. The same one I had yesterday, and the day before. We take care of that son of a bitch Harper. No employer, no contract, right?"

"We can't do that, Bob," Kate said. "Lonnie and I are cops, for God's sake. It goes wrong, somebody leaks it, and we'll all go down for conspiracy to commit murder. Now get it out of your head. You hear?"

He didn't answer, nor did he indicate that he was willing to take heed of what Kate had said, and I didn't like that worth a damn. I knew Bob Ryan better than anybody. He was a law only unto himself.

"Bob," I said, quietly. "You heard what she said?"

He scowled, turned down the corners of his mouth in an angry grimace, "Yeah, I heard her."

I stared hard at him; he stared right back, then shrugged, and picked up his cup. Me? I wasn't convinced and, by the look on her face, neither was Kate.

"So where the hell is she?" Lonnie asked.

"She must be staying in one of the local hotels," Kate said. "She could even be right under our noses."

"Tim," I said, "she must have rented a car. Can we track it? She would have rented it at the airport, right?"

"I already did that. I ran the security footage as she went through Customs and Immigration and that's where I lost her. They were real busy that day. More than a dozen international flights arrived during the thirty minutes between one-forty-five and two-fifteen. The customs hall was packed. They checked her through and she... she just disappeared."

He looked down at his laptop, then up again.

"So... I checked every car rental company operating out of Atlanta Hartsfield. None of them rented a car or any other type of vehicle to any of the five... Make that four suspects or a Calaway Jones. This girl is good, really good, but no one is perfect, right? Right! I think I may have found something." He grinned like a kid that had just been handed two scoops of Rocky Road ice cream.

"Enterprise picked up a Bettie Marlowe at International Arrivals and..." He looked around the table. "And rented her a black Mini Cooper. But here's the kicker: I could find no one by that name registered on any incoming international flight that day."

YES!

"The transaction," he continued, "is time-stamped at three-oh-three that same afternoon. I called Enterprise, but no one remembered her. The rental documents show that she had an American driver's license with an address in Valdosta, Georgia. The date of birth on the license was June 1, 1990, so she's twenty-seven years old. I ran a reverse on the address and came up with a phone number. I called it, but it went to voice mail; one of those computer-generated things. I didn't leave a message."

"That was her!" I said. And I was certain that it was.

"How d'you know?" Amanda asked.

"I've seen that car, twice. Once at the hospital and again outside these offices, on Georgia. It's her."

"You didn't say anything to me," she said, and she didn't sound happy about it.

I shrugged, "There was no reason to. It was just a car."

"If it's not her," Tim said, "I don't know what could have happened to her. People can't just... disappear... Can they?"

"Come on, Tim. You know better than that."

"Hey," he said, "how many skip searches d'you think I've done for you over the years?"

He didn't wait for an answer.

"Hundreds, maybe thousands, and I found them all. They leave a trail. The only thing I haven't done yet is run the credit card she used at Enterprise, but I will, and you know what? I won't find anything. The Israelis are damned good at what they do. If she wanted to disappear... She could. She did?" It was both a statement and a question.

I stared down the expanse of the table at him; he stared right back, shaking his head, slowly.

"Okay," I said, thinking out loud. "Maybe the car I saw was the one, maybe it wasn't. Either way, we know she met with Shady sometime after three-thirty that afternoon, so she didn't disappear. Well, not right away, and we have Shady's description of her, for what it's worth. So what would she have done when she got through with Shady? She would have traveled to Chattanooga, Right?"

No answer.

"If she did, she must have checked into a hotel, and it shouldn't be too difficult to figure out which one, right, Tim?"

He leaned back in his chair, poked at his glasses, and said, "Shouldn't be. I'll go take a look."

He'd been gone for some ten minutes when I finally decided I'd had enough of the waiting. The room, while he'd been gone, had turned into a morgue, so quiet was it. I thought about getting another cup of coffee, but I was already wired... and well, I didn't. After maybe five minutes into the wait, I saw Kate sneak her hand under the table and take hold of Bob's. He looked fondly down at her; talk about beauty and the beast. I looked sideways at Amanda. She'd seen it too, and she shrugged and smiled. Me? I'd had enough. I got up and went to join Tim.

"Well," I said, "did you find anything?"

He was still tapping away, "Just give me a minute."

Finally, he rolled his chair away from the keyboard and looked up at me.

"Nothing!"

"What?"

"What I said. Nothing. No one by the name of Jones or Marlowe has checked into any of the hotels within a thirty-mile radius of Chattanooga during the last three weeks. If she came here, she truly has disappeared."

Christ, I thought, *she really is a ghost. What the hell do we do now?*

"What about women with French names?" I asked. It was a forlorn hope, but I could think of nothing else.

"I'll give it a try."

He rolled his chair back to his console and started in on the tapping again, and that continued for what must have been another five minutes, or more. Finally, he gave up and rolled himself away again.

"Nope... Nothing that gels with what we're looking for."

"Geez, Tim. She can't have disappeared. We know she's here for Christ's sake. I've spoken to her. She must have used another name. Find her," I snapped, "and be damned quick about it." And I got up out of the chair and left him there, staring after me, his mouth wide open.

Maybe I shouldn't have taken my frustration out on him, but... oh, what the hell. I'm human too.

Ah, but then I thought better of it, "Sorry, Tim. That was uncalled for. I'm frustrated; do what you can, okay?"

He nodded, grinned, and turned again to his keyboard. *Does nothing ever bother that boy?*

"Okay," I said as I stormed back into the conference room. "She's dropped off the face of the earth. There's no record of anyone, by any of the names we have, checking into any hotel anywhere close, and that makes no damn sense. I've spoken to her, which means she has to be close enough to receive the data. We need to find her, and there's only one way to do that: old-fashioned legwork. We go hotel to hotel until we find something. We're looking for a woman of between twenty-five and thirty-five driving a black Mini Cooper that checked into a hotel sometime on or after June 30, and we have to get right on it; tonight. Are you up for it?"

They were. So we decided to divide the city into four sectors. Kate and Lonnie would go together to Rossville. Bob would take Jacque and go west. Amanda and I would take the north while Tim would search Cleveland and Dalton via computer—the Titan would stay on at all times.

***

We hit the road at just after six o'clock that evening. We left two at a time, Amanda and I being the last to leave. Again, I had it in my head that if Jones would follow anyone, it would be me, and I had to be sure that didn't happen, but how?

I decided the easiest way was to head for Erlanger Hospital—I had a good reason to visit: Ronnie was still there—that damned staph infection—and the parking system lends itself well for what I had in mind.

I drove to the hospital, keeping a sharp eye out, front and rear, for a tail; I saw none, but that meant nothing. I turned off Central Avenue into the hospital, but instead of bearing right into the multi-story, I stayed left, gunned the car up the loop, circled around the top, and slipped into a spot at the side of the road, between an SUV and Ford pickup, and we settled down to watch. And we did, for almost fifteen minutes. The black Mini never appeared.

I figured we were in the clear, but it was then that I realized that rather than the asset I'd thought the Camaro to be, it was, for now at least, more of a liability. The problem with it was that, as far as I knew, it was probably one of only maybe a dozen like it in the city. The damn thing stuck out like a sore thumb. Still, it was all I had so it would have to do, at least for now.

Did you ever have that feeling that you suddenly were under a spotlight, that all eyes were upon you? That's exactly how I felt when I drove back out onto Central that evening, and I didn't like it one damn bit.

Amanda and me, we'd drawn the north side of the city: Bonny Oaks Drive, Shallowford Road, and the Highway 153 corridor from Hamilton Place to Northgate and beyond. Easy enough, you might think, but you'd be wrong. You have no idea how many hotels and motels there are on that stretch. Not that any of the other areas would have been any better; they were all much the same.

Most of the hotel managers were compliant, even cooperative; the badge, even a PI badge, works wonders and we were, with a couple of exceptions, allowed access to the guest registries. We found maybe a half-dozen single women that might have been persons of interest, but while they fit the bill, in one form or another, most were business women, reps of one sort or another, and none of them were driving Mini Coopers.

By ten o'clock that evening, we were both just about done in. Amanda looked like she hadn't been to bed for a week, and I felt no different. By that time, we were all the way out beyond the river, almost to Hixson Pike, and I figured we had maybe a half-dozen more stops still to make. We'd already checked the Hampton Inn and were actually talking to the night manager at the Country Inn & Suites when my burner phone rang.

"Harry, it's me."

"Hey, Bob. How's it going?"

"I think I might have something. I'm at the La Quinta on Brown's Ferry Road. The night manager says they have a student staying with them, a female, twenty-two, from England. She checked in on the evening of June 30. Yeah, yeah, I know. She's too young, right? But get this, Harry; she's driving a black Mini Cooper S."

"Hell yeah!" I said. "That's just west of the mountain, less than a mile from the house, as the crow flies. Has to be her. Have you approached her yet?"

"No, I figured I'd call you first; see how you want to handle it."

"Good. Sit tight. Don't do anything until I get there. I'll call Kate and have her call in some backup. We're on our way."

**

Inside her room on the ground floor of the La Quinta Inn & Suites Chattanooga, Calaway Jones was listening to her police scanner as she stuffed her clothing into her rollaway. She had, so she thought, maybe five minutes before the first police units arrived, always provided that there were

182

none close by, but even then she wasn't too bothered. She'd planned for such a contingency and had driven her escape route a half-dozen times. It took her less than three minutes to stuff her belongings into the rollaway, shove the Beretta into the holster on her waist and slip out of the rear door of the hotel. The Mini Cooper was parked out back, on the lot in front of the China Gourmet restaurant, as close to the hotel door as she could have possibly gotten it.

She hit the unlock button on the key fob, wrenched the door open, flung the rollaway inside, slid into the seat, hit the starter, slammed the gear shift into reverse, circled back a half-car length, then rammed the car into first gear, and squealed away in a tight circle around the south end of the mini mall and the Chinese restaurant. As she hurtled toward the restaurant, she caught sight of a brown Dodge Ram truck as it too burned rubber and came after her.

She almost laughed aloud. She'd had an idea someone might be out there watching, and she was delighted that the driver of the truck had played right into her hands. Had he stayed where he was, he would have seen her circle around the back of the mini mall and back out into the parking lot. Had he stayed put, he could have followed her out onto Brown's Ferry Road where she made a hard left and headed for Elder Mountain. The heavy pickup truck was no match for the Cooper, and she was away on Brown's Ferry even before he'd rounded the north end of the mall, back to the parking lot.

Knowing she had the edge on the big truck, she slowed a little, to make sure the driver saw the direction she was headed. Then she hit the gas and rode the car hard to Adkins where she hung a hard left, then gunned the car to Isbell where she turned left again to Kelly's Ferry Road.

She glanced at the rearview mirror; there was no sign of the truck, and she smiled as she made a right onto Kelly's and continued on at a much more sedate speed to Highway 41 and then on to Halestown where she turned east onto I-24, then south onto I-59 into Georgia. It was a long and circuitous route, but she wasn't bothered. It kept her well away from the police activity she knew, from listening to her scanner, to be concentrated in the vicinity of the Brown's Ferry/I-24 junction.

A little more than thirty minutes later she was parked outside the rented vacation cabin in Rising Fawn, Georgia, off West Brow Road on Lookout Mountain, some fourteen miles to the south of the Starke residence on East Brow Road.

Chapter 17
Friday, July 14, 11pm

"How the hell did she know?" I was so angry I could barely see straight.

"How should I know, for Christ's sake?" Bob growled. He was just about as PO'd as I was.

"Hell, if we hadn't been sitting right where we were, watching her damned car, we'd have missed her altogether."

"Might as well have," I said, angrily. "She's long gone, and we have no damned idea where she went or where she is now. Damn, damn, *dammit!* Tell me what happened, Bob. Did you get a look at her?"

Apparently, Bob had followed the Mini Cooper out onto Brown's Ferry Road, but by the time he was able to floor the gas pedal, she was away around the bend, and he didn't see her again. He figured he must have been halfway to Elder Mountain before he realized she'd duped him, doubled back somewhere. He'd arrived back at the hotel just as I pulled into the parking lot behind Kate and Lonnie.

"No. I didn't see her; not really, just a glimpse. She came out of the rear door like a damned rabbit, fast, and she took off over there," he pointed to the south end of the mini mall. "I should have known. Hell, I've been doing this shit long enough. She went round the back of the strip. Where could she go? All I had to do was sit still and wait for her to reappear. I could have had her..."

Oh, he was upset; more than I could ever remember, and rightly so. He'd made a stupid, rookie mistake, but what the hell? In the heat of the moment... Hindsight, however, is always twenty-twenty, right?

"So what the hell do we do now?" he asked, as he took a wild kick at the front driver's side tire of his Ram.

And that was indeed the question, and it was one to which I had no immediate answer. It was, in fact, going to be a long night.

We questioned the La Quinta night manager and his staff. None of them had seen more than a glimpse of the elusive young student, ostensibly in Chattanooga to study the American Civil War and visit the battlefields.

She'd registered under the name Mary Sutton and looked to be no more than the twenty-two years old stated on her driver's license. She was, so they all agreed, slim, five eight or nine with short brown hair that framed a face that none of them had seen long enough to be able to recognize even if they saw her again.

The damned ghost has ridden in and ridden out again, and nobody has a damned clue what she really looks like.

We were, the six of us, standing together in a group outside the front of the hotel. The parking lot was ablaze with flashing blue and red lights.

I didn't blame Bob. There was no doubt in my mind that Calaway Jones had been at least one jump ahead of us all along, and had been well-prepared for just such a contingency. The fact that Bob had reacted the way he had was just... one of those things. Would I have played it differently? If I was honest with myself, probably not. The problem was, however, that Jones was in the wind and she wouldn't give us a second chance to grab her... unless... But the hour was late, and I was tired and in no mood to think it through. I needed sleep in the worst way. Jacque, so it seemed, thought so too.

"I think it's time we all went home," she said. "I don't know about y'all, but I gotta get some sleep."

"I agree," I said. "There's nothing more we can do tonight. I don't think she'll check into another hotel, at least not anywhere close; she's too smart for that. We'll meet at our place in the morning for..." I looked at Amanda; she nodded. "For breakfast and to consider our options. Nine o'clock be okay?"

It was, and with that, we went our separate ways. Amanda and me to the top of the mountain; Kate climbed up beside Bob in the Ram, and Lonnie agreed to take Jacque home to Wendy. It had been one hell of a day, and I was glad to see the back of it.

It was just after midnight when Amanda and I said goodnight to my crew and the members of Chattanooga's finest and headed home.

I hadn't been in the house more than a couple of minutes when I realized I was ravenously hungry. While Amanda poured drinks for two, I made a ham sandwich on French bread that would have choked a horse. There must have been at least a half-pound of Black Forest in that thing. Whatever; it and a half-pint of red put me right at ease... Nah, not really.

Amanda headed to the bedroom to "change into something comfortable," and I dimmed the lights and dumped myself down, sandwich in hand, on the sofa in front of the picture window. The view was, as always, spectacular, and as I looked out over the city I was able to relax, some, but I couldn't get the sneaky bitch out of my head. How the hell had she known we were onto her? Not a one of us had a smartphone, at least one that had a battery in it. The only thing I could think of was that she must have had a police scanner.

"I have a gift for you," Amanda said when she returned.

"Oh?" I looked up at her. She was standing in front of me, her back to the window. She was wearing only a T-shirt that barely covered her... She had her hands on her hips, her feet just far enough apart for me to see the jeweled lights of the city between her legs. She reminded me of Peter Pan… but oh so much sexier.

"What gift?"

And then it dropped, "Ohhh! Nice. Thank you, but…"

"What do you mean, *but?*"

"Nothing. Come sit with me for a minute." I put the last of my sandwich on the side table and patted the spot beside me.

She sat. I put my arm around her; pulled her close to me; took her chin between my fingers and tilted her head so that I could look into her eyes. "I so love you," I said, at last, and I kissed her, gently, and I put every ounce of my heart and soul into it, and she knew it.

"Hey," she said, as I kissed her eyelids. "I love you too, but this is not like you. You never… What's it all about?"

The truth was, I'd had one of those moments; one of those moments when it all brims uncontrollably over the top. I don't think until that moment I'd ever realized just how much I really did love her.

I shrugged, "I love you," I said, simply.

"Oh, Harry. What's going on in there? Tell me, please."

The problem was, I couldn't, not really. I knew something she didn't, and I couldn't tell her, because… How the hell do you tell the person you love that's she's under a death sentence without scaring her stupid? You can't. So I didn't.

"Nothing. I was just thinking that I'd like to unwrap my gift, right here, right now."

And I did. And what a gift it was.

Chapter 18
Saturday, July 15, 9am

I was up early the following morning, Saturday, well before daylight, and I sat out on the patio in my boxers and watched the sun come up. As you know, my usual morning routine includes a two-mile run, but with things being the way they were, and not knowing where the b… Calaway Jones might be, I figured that it probably wasn't a good idea.

By five o'clock, the sun was already up, and I was on my second cup of coffee when Amanda slipped into the pool wearing nothing but her skin.

For several minutes I watched as she swam slow laps of the pool until finally, she rested her arms on the apron in front of me.

"Come on, Harry. It's lovely. Please."

So I did. I slipped out of my boxers, took a header over the top of her, turned, swam underwater to where she was still leaning on the apron, slipped my arms around her waist and nuzzled her neck.

"Oh my," she giggled. "What a big boy you are."

Have you ever made love in deep water? If not, you should try it. I can recommend it. My only advice is, don't get too carried away. I nearly drowned my silly self.

They all arrived early. Fortunately, though, by then we'd showered and dressed, and Amanda had a couple of pounds of bacon cooked, biscuits in the oven, and a pan full of gravy on the range. I had made a half-gallon of Gori Gesha Forest coffee and was already on my second cup when Bob and Kate arrived.

We ate breakfast out on the patio. Not because we couldn't talk inside the house - we could - but because the weather was perfect. The temperature up there on the mountain was always ten degrees cooler than it was down in the city. The air was crisp, and a light breeze was blowing; it was one of those days you were glad to be alive... *But for how long?* I wondered.

I helped Amanda clear away the plates, and I made another pot of coffee and carried it on a tray with an assortment of cookies back outside.

"Okay," Bob said, "I've had enough of this crap. What the hell are we going to do about this... this... woman?"

I'd thought long and hard overnight about that, and I'd been able to come up with only one answer.

"It's me she want's, so that's the way we have to play it."

"Oh no," Amanda said. "No, no, *no!*"

"It's okay," I said. "It's the only way. She has an agenda... She... is playing head games... with me, and she's using everybody here to do it. The shot she took at you—your Lexus—Ronnie, the smiley faces; it's all aimed at me. She figures she can mess with my head and I'll make mistakes, and to an extent, she's right. You guys are my life, and she knows that. There's only one way to stop her, and that's to take the initiative. We, that is I, have to go on the offensive."

"And just how the hell do you think you're going to do that?" Amanda asked. Oh, she was angry.

"Hey," I said, "calm down. I'm not going to do anything stu–"

It was at that moment Kate's burner phone rang. I looked at her, my eyebrows raised in question.

She looked at the screen, then at me and shrugged, "It's Chief Johnston. I had to give him my number. I couldn't be out of touch; not completely, besides: you never know when we might need some heavy help." She answered the call.

"Hey, Chief. What's up?"

She listened intently, her eyes narrowed. She looked at me as she listened. She bit her lower lip, and slowly shook her head. I got the idea that she wasn't believing what she was hearing. The call lasted maybe two minutes, and though I couldn't

193

hear what he was saying, I could hear the chief's voice the whole time he was talking, and I could tell he was either angry or extremely alarmed about something. Finally, she thanked him, said goodbye, and disconnected.

She sighed, picked up her cup, sipped on it, and then stared down into the liquid.

"Well?" I said. "Are you going to tell us, or what?"

She looked up at me, then she turned to look at Bob, and the look she gave him would have turned a lesser man to stone, and he caught it.

"What?" he asked, frowning at her.

"Little Billy Harper is dead," she told him through tight lips. "What the hell have you done, Bob?"

"Me? ME? Nothing. What do you mean, he's dead?"

Oh yeah. I wanted to hear that too.

"He was shanked going to the shower last night. He was stabbed eleven times, and his throat was cut. Did you do it, Bob? Did you make a call? Because if you did, we're done, and I'll take you in myself."

She was on the edge of her seat, ready to do just that.

"Hey, hey," I said. "Hold on, Kate." I turned to Bob.

"Tell me you didn't do this."

His face was white. His hands clenched into fists.

"You have to ask me that?" he asked, quietly. "I told you I wouldn't, and I didn't. I don't lie to you, or anybody else, Harry. I didn't do it. Now you either believe me, both of you," he looked at Kate, "or you don't. And if you don't... well, screw you. I'm outa here," and he rose to his feet.

"Sit down, Bob," I said. "I believe you."

He looked at Kate. She stared up at him, then nodded. He sat down again.

"So," Kate said. "You didn't do it. Then who did?" She looked at Lonnie.

"You?" she asked.

"*What?* What the hell do you think?" He asked, indignantly. "You think I did it? You must think I'm stupid. We're talking murder here. Any one of a dozen people could have done it. Hell, you know how many people that piece of crap screwed over during his lifetime. There must be a couple of hundred people that hated him enough to have done it; some of 'em are residing right alongside him in USP, and you ask me if I done it? Screw you, Kate... Lieutenant. You think I did it; prove it."

"Oh, I will..."

"Stop," I said. "This is getting us nowhere. Bob said he didn't do it, and so did Lonnie. That's good enough. Let's move on." *Oh yeah. Bob said he didn't, but Lonnie never did quite say that.*

I looked him in the eye. He held my gaze, a half-smile on his lips and... he winked at me. *Son of a bitch!*

I looked at Kate. She was looking at Bob. She didn't see it. I looked again at Lonnie. He leaned back in his chair and stared stoically out over the city.

"Harry," Amanda said, "if Harper is dead, surely that means... that..."

I took her hand and squeezed it.

"I sure as hell hope so."

"So... so, what do we do?" she asked.

I thought about it, then said, "She has a phone, and I have the number. Shady gave it to me. I'll call her."

I got up and went into the house to get my iPhone and the phone number and then returned to my seat. I slipped the battery back into the phone and tapped in the number.

She answered on the third ring.

"Hello, Harry. I had an idea you might call. I have some news for you... but I think you may already know. My, how fast bad news—or good news—travels. Anyway, I had a call from Lester Tree, Shady, I think you call him. He told me about your conversation, and he also told me something else, something very interesting... to both of us. It seems that his employer, and mine, Gordon Harper, is dead. Did you know that, Harry?"

"Yeah, I know he's dead, and I know who you are. You're ex-Mossad, an assassin. Look, I know that Harper hired you to kill me, and I know you've been playing games, and I know why. Hell, you told me yourself... Look, so far you've managed to scare the crap out of my wife and wound one of my people, but now you can stop it. He's dead, so I assume that you don't have to go through with it; you can call it off. Right?"

"Oh yes, he hired me to do more than just kill you... but you're right, Harry, well, somewhat. Now that he's gone all of that stupid extra stuff he wanted done really doesn't matter anymore, does it?"

"You're calling it off?"

"You know I can't do that, Harry. He paid me up front, well, half. I can't break a contract. That wouldn't be good for business, now would it? No, you're still a dead man, Harry. The rest of the contract... well, I didn't get paid for that, so I'll let it slide, which means Amanda and your friends are off the hook, but only if they stay out of it. They don't... well, we don't want to think about that, now do we?"

It wasn't everything I wanted to hear, but to know that Amanda and the others were safe was a relief. But if I told you I was happy about my own situation, I'd be lying.

"So what now?" I asked.

"I'll be looking for you, Harry. Awaiting my opportunity. One day, two days, a week. Who knows. I have all the time in the world. How about you?"

"Where are you, Calaway?"

She laughed, a tinkling gurgling laugh, sexy, but somehow menacing.

"Close. Closer than you think. Bye, Harry. See you soon." She disconnected.

I took the battery out of the phone and set it down on the table.

"Well," I said, brightly, which I didn't feel. "You guys are safe, but she still wants me."

"What?" Amanda said. "But Harper's dead. Why would she still want to kill you?"

"I guess business is business. She was paid up front, so…"

"Christ," Bob growled. "What the hell are we dealing with?"

"You? Nothing. As far as she's concerned, you're no longer a part of her contract and as long as you stay out of it, you're safe, all of you. Which is fine with me. I'll deal with her myself."

"The hell you will…"

"Yes, Bob. The hell I will. Not you. Not Lonnie. Not Kate. Me, and me alone. You got that?"

"Harry…"

"No, Amanda. I mean it. I have to do it myself. I can do this. We've been overthinking it. It's simple. I'm going to give her what she wants: me. No, Amanda, I'm not going to simply hand myself over. I'll dangle the bait and hope she bites. If she does…"

"Sheesh, Harry," Bob said, shaking his head. "I don't like it. What if she catches you when you're not ready? She won't give you a second chance."

I shrugged, "Then I can't let that happen." *And just how the hell d'you think you're going to manage that?* I asked myself. *You need to let 'em help.* I was thinking and shaking my head at the same time.

"What are you thinking, Harry?" Kate asked.

"Nothing. I was just running through my options. It's okay. I can handle it."

"Fine," she said. "At least talk it through with us…"

"No," I said. "If I do that, you'll stick your noses in. I need a clear head. I don't want to be worrying about you guys. She said for you to stay out of it. That's what you'll do. No arguments. Now, if you don't mind, I need to spend some time with Amanda. I'll see you all at the office on Monday."

***

I spent the rest of the day with Amanda, most of it quietly by the pool. Amanda tried several times to get me to talk about my plan, but it didn't happen. For one thing, I didn't have one, for another, I just didn't want to talk about it; I wanted to think. How the hell was I going to draw this maniac out, and to my advantage? The only answer I could come up with was that I stop hiding from her.

I knew she had to be watching me, waiting… *For what? A chance to take a shot at me? She can't do that while I'm hidden away here at home. Okay, so I need to get out of here.*

I looked at my watch. It was after nine o'clock, getting dark. *"Closer than you think," is what she said. What does that mean?* I wondered.

We were out on the patio, by the pool. I went to the wall that separated the property from East Brow, dragged up a chair, and climbed up onto it, I looked up and down the road: nothing. I climbed down again, returned the chair to the table, sat down on it and picked up my glass.

"Anything?" Amanda asked.

I shook my head. "No, but that doesn't mean she's not out there somewhere; she is, down there, maybe." I nodded in the direction of the terrace

200

wall that separated the patio from the gardens that stretched away down the mountain a hundred yards or so to a second, perimeter wall.

"Surely not." She stretched up in her chair, trying to see down the slope; she couldn't, not without...

"Don't," I said, as she started to get up. "If she is there, you won't see her, but she'll see you. Stay put."

Somehow, though, I had it my mind that she wasn't down there. I figured it wasn't her style to go creeping about in the undergrowth. She was more the "walk quickly up behind you and put two in the back of your head type," or she would go for a long shot with the M400. No, I figured she'd watch and wait for her chance. *How would I do it if it was me?*

Hmmm, there are really only two ways down the mountain: Ochs Highway and Scenic Highway. If she's been watching us since she got here two weeks ago, she'd know which one we, I, use most often; Scenic. All she has to do... Okay, maybe that will work. I wonder if she's still listening in. If she is... Can't hurt to try. I need to make a call.

I called Bob using my burner phone.

"Hey," I said. "I need a favor."

"You got it."

"I'm gonna try and draw this bitch out of hiding. I'm going to have Amanda call you in the morning, on her iPhone. She's going to tell you a story. I want you to play along, okay? All you have to do is say, 'I'm on it. I'm heading out right now,' or some such, and then hang up. And then you stay put. I don't want any of you out there while I'm doing this. You could get hurt, or worse. Does that work for you?"

He said he did, and I disconnected, sat back in my chair and stared down at the glittering lights of the city. It was going to be a long night.

Chapter 19
Sunday, July 16, 5am

I woke as usual at five the following morning, Sunday. I showered, dressed in jeans, a black T-shirt and sneakers. Then I made coffee for two and took them back to the bedroom; Amanda was sitting up in bed, waiting. Neither one of us had slept more than a couple of hours. I'd explained the nub of my plan to her, but I hadn't gone into detail. She'd have flipped if she'd known what I was going to do... and anyway, it might not work. I was taking a whole lot for granted, and it all had to come together. If not... well, that didn't bear thinking about.

It being Sunday, I was in no hurry. I had to give Calaway time to get out and about, although I had no doubt that she was an early riser too. I had to make what I was about to do appear to be part of my normal routine, believable.

At eight-thirty we ate bagels together, drank another cup of coffee, and I began to get ready.

I strapped on my ankle holster, checked the Glock 26—my ankle piece—and then took the heavy Spider tactical vest from the closet, checked the ceramic plates in the sleeves, chest, and back and then climbed into it. It felt like I was wearing a straitjacket. I checked the Heckler & Koch VP9, made sure there was one in the chamber, screwed the suppressor onto the barrel, then slid it into its holster on my belt. I slipped two full, fifteen-round mags into the pockets of the vest, and the I put on a lightweight, black golf jacket. I was ready to go.

I looked at my watch. It was nine-twenty-five. I finished the dregs of what must have been my fifth cup of coffee, then I went out to the garage, opened the doors and the gate, and started the ZL1. I stood for a moment, listening to the low growl of the engine; it was somehow reassuring. I smiled bitterly and went back into the kitchen where Amanda was waiting, her iPhone in one hand and the battery in the other.

I looked at my watch, took a deep breath, and nodded. She inserted the battery and made the call. I leaned in close and listened.

"Amanda, what the hell are you doing calling me on your iPhone?" Bob sounded pissed.

"I had to. I panicked. I couldn't find the other stupid phone. Bob, Harry's gone. You've got to do something. He said he was going to the office, but... he's by himself. If he..."

"I got it," he said. "I'm on it. Turn that damned phone off and take out the battery; you hear?" And he hung up. I grabbed her, hugged her, kissed her, and ran out to the car. I reversed out onto the road and headed for Scenic Highway...

As I drove down the mountain, I turned off the burner phone and took out the battery. Knowing Amanda, I was certain the minute I left the house, she'd be on the phone to Tim. If the phone was dead, he couldn't track it.

I drove the speed limit, where I could. There are places on Scenic Highway where even twenty miles an hour is too fast.

I kept my eyes on the rearview mirror, and I watched the front and both sides of the road, looking for that black Mini until finally, I hit Cummings Highway and then Broad Street: nothing. *Damn, I could have sworn... Where the hell is she?*

I drove along Broad at a leisurely speed, keeping a close watch all around: still nothing. And then I spotted something. To my right, parked between two cars in front of Bell's Smoke Shop, was a black Mini. It had been reversed into the spot: *so the driver could see the road? Maybe.*

I could see the windshield, but as far as I could tell there was no one inside. I swung the Camaro right into the east end of the parking lot, and as I did, the Mini rocketed out of its spot, its tires smoking, and then without stopping made a hard right onto Broad and accelerated at high speed toward the overpass. *Holy Crap. That's her.*

I followed, riding the gas pedal—damn that car was responsive—and made it out onto Broad just in time to see the tail end of the Mini make a right onto 25th. *She's heading for the Interstate, by God. If she is, I've got her.*

She was. By the time she made the left turn onto Long Street, I was less than fifty yards behind her and gaining fast.

She hit the on-ramp and gunned the Mini up onto I-24 heading south. For almost a mile we weaved from lane to lane, dodging the slower moving vehicles. Slowly but surely, I gained on her. When we reached the Fourth Avenue Exit I was right on her tail, less than five yards behind her... *Gotcha, you bitch!*

Back when I was a cop I was trained in the Pit Maneuver, the quick way to end a high-speed chase, and that was what I was about to do.

I pulled to the right of the Mini, gunned the engine, and came up with my left fender to her right rear. In the heads-up display on the windshield, the speed was hovering around ninety-three miles an hour, a little faster than I would have liked, but what the hell. I put my left fender to the Mini and pulled down on the steering wheel, and pushed. The Mini began to break away, to slide sideways away from me. It was working.

What she did next totally blindsided me. Oh, she was good. The damn Mini, instead of sliding sideways into the concrete barriers, did a perfect three-sixty, ending up behind me. Now she was tailing me. *Sheeit!*

I slammed on the brakes; she pulled to my right and rocketed past me and away. As she drew level, I glanced to my right; the Mini's windows were tinted; I couldn't see her. I stamped on the gas pedal, pushing it to the floor. The engine howled as the supercharger kicked in and I was slammed back into the seat. In what seemed to be no more than a second I was almost alongside her left fender. I was about to apply the Pit again, but she swerved to the right, onto the East Ridge off ramp and I almost didn't make it. I hit the brakes, wrenched the wheel hard to the right, hit the gas and heard the tires squeal as I rocketed onto the ramp after her.

She was a pro, and smart. That little car was no match for the ZL on the highway but on the streets... well, I was about to find out.

She hurtled down the ramp and without slowing careened onto Westside Drive, heading toward East Ridge. I expected her to push on through the tunnel to Ringgold Road. If she did, I had her. Surprise, surprise; she didn't. Instead, she hit the brakes, came almost to a complete stop—I had to swerve to the right to avoid hitting her— and I watched her in my rear-view mirror as she made a hard left onto Elder Street. *Damn, damn, DAMN!*

I screeched to a stop, slammed the gearshift into reverse, backed up, and followed her onto Elder. She was already out of sight, but I knew there was nowhere for her to go except forward. I hit the gas, and the Camaro hurtled along the narrow street, bucking and swaying like a damned hydroplane, but it was there the Camaro came into its own. It clung to the road like a limpet, cornering like a Formula 1 race car at Monaco. Thank God it was Sunday morning, and moving traffic was all but non-existent because I know from the heads-up display that I hit eighty in at least two places... and I caught her. I saw her brake lights flicker as she approached the stop sign at Old Ringgold Road and then she was gone again.

I followed her, over the Interstate. I thought I'd lost her, but as I rounded the curve onto the long straight that was Old Ringgold, I saw the brake lights flickering as she slowed.

I hit the gas and was up on her tail in just seconds... but she was ready for me. She made a hard right onto Anderson and headed for the McCauley campus. I smiled as I hit the gas and followed tight on her ass. I was home again. I'd spent six years on campus at McCauley and knew exactly what lay ahead. *Dead end, you stupid bitch.*

The road dead-ended in a parking lot behind the school, She made a left into the lot and hit the gas; I was right on her tail. She must have been doing more than forty miles an hour when she executed a perfect, high-speed one-eighty hand-brake turn. I would have done the same, had I known the car better than I did. The hand/parking brake in that growler was nothing more than a button on the center console. It could happen, but I wasn't sure how to do it. So I hit the brakes, swung the car to the right, wrenched the wheel hard to the left, and hit the gas; the tires screamed as the back end of the car slid violently into the turn. Not as quick as the Mini, but not bad considering how long I'd been driving the Camaro.

I followed her back onto Anderson. She was now almost two blocks ahead of me, and again I saw the tail lights flicker as she made a sliding right onto Dodds Avenue and then a hard left onto Kirby.

She had me there. The big car was no match for the Mini on the tight corners. By the time I'd made the turn onto Kirby she was four blocks ahead of me; I caught the flash of her brake lights as she made another sharp left onto South Lyerly... and that's where I lost her. I fishtailed onto Lyerly; there was no sign of her. She'd disappeared. *Holy crap. Where the hell did she go?*

I cruised slowly along Lyerly toward the junction of East Twelfth. *Where the hell could she be? Hell, I wasn't that far behind her.*

I was on the back side of the old Stewart Mills plant, where the road split. I could turn right onto the continuation of Anderson or I could continue on Lyerly; I continued on Lyerly keeping the plant to my left. The old mill complex had been vacant for years, fenced off and derelict. I passed an open gate in the fence, noted the three huge round tanks, rusting now and... *The gate's open. The frigging gate's open.*

I screeched to a stop, slammed the car into reverse and backed up. Yeah, the gate was open all right, but there was no Mini. *Damn!*

I cruised on along Lyerly to East Twelfth and turned left, skirting the perimeter fence of the plant. I was now at its west end. The main gate into the compound was at the center of the perimeter fence, set back maybe twelve feet to give access to what once had been a brick guard shack, and there it was. The Mini was pulled in tight up against the gate, its hood right up to the crumbling brick wall of the guard shack. If I hadn't been looking for it, I might well have missed it.

I pulled up behind the Mini, blocking it in. I turned off the motor, exited the Camaro, pulled the VP9 from its holster, and slowly approached the rear of the car; the gun leveled at the passenger-side window. The driver was gone. I looked around: nothing. Then I noticed there were dusty shoe prints all over the hood. *She's inside the damn compound. She used the Mini to climb over the fence. So, is this the end of the trail?*

I stared through the wire into the compound, thinking: *What if I hadn't seen her at the smoke shop? She sure as hell would have seen me, and she'd have tailed me to the office where... Well, who knows what. As it was, it was me that had tailed her. I'd had the upper hand. At least I did until I lost her. So now what?*

The old plant beyond the gate was a forlorn, forgotten place, and she was somewhere in there, inside the compound, maybe even inside the building, and on foot. She was going nowhere, that was for sure, but what the hell was she up to? She had the advantage. *She's waiting... waiting for me to go in there after her? Bad move, Harry. Don't do it. Don't go in there. Call Kate. Ask her to bring backup. No! There's no time. If I dither around out here, she'll be gone before backup can get here. I have to finish this, one way or the other, now.*

I climbed on the hood of the Mini and looked around the open compound. It stretched north and south maybe two hundred and fifty feet from South Lyerly to South Watkins, and maybe sixty feet from the gate to the plant wall, and it was all wide open space. If she was in there somewhere, waiting... *Ah, what the hell.*

I clambered up onto the top of the fence, then the brick wall, and jumped down inside. I crouched, waiting, listening, the VP9 in a two-handed grip, ready: nothing. I heard nothing, not even outside on the street. Hell, it was almost scary; not even the birds were singing. All was quiet. *Come on, Harry; get over it. It's Sunday morning for Pete's sake.*

I jumped upright and ran as hard as I could to the wall of the building and flattened myself against it, and again I waited and listened, and again I heard nothing. One thing I knew for sure: I couldn't stay where I was. Me in black against a white wall in bright sunlight? Think about it.

I'd noticed that there was no way around the building to the south, so I decided to go north, toward Lyerly. Staying close against the wall, I eased my way north until I came to the northwest corner of the building and what might have been a creek but was, in fact, a man-made storm drain: wide and deep: no easy way across. I peered around the corner: long grass, a huge square pond, a water tower, more buildings, more open space.

She has to be there somewhere, damn it. There ain't no other way out. Now I know what it must feel like for those soldiers in Fallujah, like a rat heading into a trap.

I had to do it. But first I had to get across that damned storm drain. I looked to my left and spotted a concrete bridge that I figured must provide access to the area beyond the north wall of the building: easy enough, but it would put me out in the open. I'd be exposed and vulnerable. I hesitated, but I had no choice; it was that way or no way.

I slid the VP9 into its holster, took a deep breath and dodged across the dozen or so yards to the bridge and then crossed it, turned east, and sprinted hard for the water tower, expecting any second to feel the bullets slam into me, but no. I made it to the tower, stopped, looked quickly around: there was no cover. The legs of the tower were steel, angle iron, no more than six or eight inches. *Where the hell is she?*

I heard gravel crunch, and I spun around and there she was, gun in hand; not at all what I'd expected. Yes, she looked young, ridiculously young, but there was an air of confidence about her. The stance was casual, languid, even. She was slim, boyish, in fact, dressed in form-fitting jeans, sneakers, and a black tee under a short tan leather jacket, and she was smiling, and I honestly think she was amused: her eyes had a sparkle in them.

"Harry Starke, I presume." She took a half-step forward, the gun never wavered. "Well, here we are at last. Now what?"

"Give it up, Calaway. Quit now, while you can, before you get killed or end up in prison for the rest of your days."

She laughed, "Better men than you, Harry. I was trained by the best... and, anyway, you're not as young as you were, now are you. What are you, forty-six, forty-seven? You do look good, though."

"It's over," I said. "The police are on the way. They'll be here in a matter of minutes. You've nowhere to go." I watched her eyes; they never left mine. *Hell, she looks young enough to be my daughter.*

"So you say." She paused, shook her head, and looked at me as if she was exasperated. "What do you think I am, Harry? Even if what you say is true, do you truly think I couldn't find a way out of this..." She waved the gun in the air, an all-encompassing gesture. "Out of this relic of capitalism at its worst?" She gazed around at the vast, abandoned building and its surroundings, taking in the rusted fuel tanks, silos, graffiti, the garbage, the broken crates, the filth.

"Can you imagine having to spend your life working in a place like this? I can't... but I digress. I don't believe you, Harry. You're a lone wolf and... you're a softy; you care—about your friends, your wife, especially your wife. And that makes you weak. In fact, I'd be willing to bet that right now there's not a soul knows where you are. Am I right?"

She continued to stare into my eyes. I didn't answer. I didn't need to. She knew.

"I... thought so," she said. "So it's just you and me then. Good odds, for me at least. For you, eh, not so good. How is it they say here in America? Ah yes; I seem to 'have the drop on you.'" The smile hardened, became a snarl; her eyes narrowed.

"Well," she said, "I've enjoyed fooling around with you, but I think the time has come..."

I dove sideways, rolling, twisting. I heard the suppressed Beretta crack twice: the first bullet ripped through the sleeve of my jacket; the second threw sharp shards of concrete into my face.

By the time she'd fired a third shot, I was out of her line of sight, behind a low wall that formed what once might have been a containment pool at the base of the water tower, and I thanked God it was empty.

I lay flat on the ground, the wall wasn't much—maybe two feet high at best—but it was all I had. I waited, and I listened. Nothing. All was quiet. I slid the VP9 out of its holster and lifted my head and peered over the top. She was gone; there was no sign of her, and I hadn't heard a sound. *Oh shit! Where the hell is she?*

I waited. The worst thing I could do was go looking for her. I had to make her come to me.

I jumped to my feet, leaped out from behind the tank, ran no more than ten feet to an ancient dumpster and flung myself forward. I planned to put the dumpster between her and me, but as I dropped, I felt the wind of a slug—shit, I heard the damn thing whine past my head. It couldn't have missed my neck by more than an inch or so.

She somehow had circled around and gotten behind me. She was out in the open, maybe seventy-five yards away, walking quickly toward me, both hands outstretched, the Beretta pointed straight at me.

I rolled onto my back, the VP9 clasped in both hands and—damn it—just as I unloaded five at her, she dove sideways behind a stack of rusting steel barrels, firing as she went. The first bullet clipped me. I felt the slug crease the skin of my left hip below the vest, and it burned red hot. The other two shots missed, but not by much, and I had a sudden God-awful feeling of certainty that I was outclassed and about to die.

I lay on my back, tight against the steel wall of the dumpster. I was in trouble, and I knew it. God only knew how many shots she had left. I'd counted seven; that left at least six; more, depending on the model—subcompact or full size—but she'd also have at least one spare mag, of that I was sure. Too many. Somehow, I either had to put her away or disarm her.

I had ten left in the mag and fifteen more in the spare. The problem was, though, that she was like a damned wraith. She was so fast on her feet I couldn't get a clear shot at her. And now she was gone again. Now I knew what it felt like to be the hunted. I didn't know if the bitch was playing with me, or not. But the situation was rapidly getting out of hand. One thing I knew for sure: I couldn't stay where I was. I was behind the dumpster and exposed on two sides: the left and the rear.

I looked around, spotted an opening in the building, a half open overhead roller door. I took a deep breath, rolled to my left, up onto my feet, and ran for the opening, fully expecting to run into a hail of fire... but I didn't. Nothing.

I ran out of the sunlight into the semi-darkness of the abandoned building and dove for the floor;

still nothing. I rolled sideways, leaped to my feet, crouched, looked quickly around. I was alone... at least I thought I was. I backed slowly along the wall of filthy windows, covering the area with the VP9. One minute, two, four... And then I thought the world had ended.

Three shots slammed into my chest. I felt like I'd been hit with a sledgehammer, three times. All three 9mm hollow points slammed into the ceramic plates in the vest, and I was hurled backward. The VP9 flew out of my hand, and me? I went backward through the window in a shower of broken glass.

The drop was only six, maybe eight, feet, but I landed hard, on my back. The padded vest took some of the heat out of the fall, but I was still winded, and how the hell I didn't get my throat cut, I have no idea. My left wrist and both thighs were hit by flying pieces of broken glass.

For a moment, I lay there, bleeding like a stuck pig. I pulled a shard the size of a large kitchen knife from my upper left thigh. Then I struggled to my knees, checked the other wounds and found that I'd gotten lucky. I'd sustained some nasty cuts, but nothing that was likely to cause me to bleed out, for then at least.

I stared up at the window. I saw movement. I forced myself to my feet, dove to the wall under the window and grabbed for my ankle piece, the little Glock 26.

My chest felt as if an anvil had fallen on it. I could barely breathe. My jeans were soaked with blood; my left wrist was throbbing, and the bullet crease to my hip was on fire.

I flattened my back against the wall. I watched the window; nothing. *Smartass. No, she's careful; she won't lean out. She won't make that mistake. She'll come looking for me. What the hell am I going to do?*

I edged my way slowly along the wall, trying to make as little noise as possible. I came to a doorway, set back in the wall, a small porch. The steel door was locked. *Damn!*

I looked at the Glock and sighed. Yes, it was an accurate little gun. Practicing at the range, I could easily put ten in a three-inch group at seven yards. But I wasn't at the range, there was no way I could get within twenty yards of her, let alone seven, and ten shots was all I had. I was also hurting so bad I could barely stand it. Not only that, I have big hands, and could wrap only two fingers around the grip; it wasn't at all comfortable.

I waited in the doorway and listened. Nothing. I must have been there five minutes, maybe more, before I heard a soft crunch of what I figured must be a foot on the gravel. The sound was so small, I wondered if I might have imagined it. Then I heard it again. *She must be outside the building, at the east end.*

If she was out in the open, I knew it had to be a shot of maybe forty yards or more. Again, I looked at the Baby Glock and shook my head. At that distance, and under fire, it was an almost impossible shot. But what about her?

I'd counted seven shots, plus the three that had hit me. That left at least three in the mag, but did it? If it were me, at that point I would swap the mag for a full one. This woman was a pro, so I had to assume she'd do no less.

I two-handed the Glock, straightened my arms so the gun was down by my knees, took a deep breath, and then charged out across the open space between the two buildings, sprinting as fast as I could. Thirty yards away I heard the suppressed crack of the Beretta, and as I ran, I counted. She was shooting fast: one,two,three,four,five... I dove and rolled and came up shooting, and I got lucky. I managed to get only one shot off, but it hit her.

She yelped, spun on her heel, her right arm flying wide, the Beretta spinning through the air. Then she was running, her right hand at her waist in front of her. I'd managed to clip her, but was it enough to stop her? I had a feeling I was about to find out.

I ran after her—it wasn't until later, much later, that I realized how stupid that was. I ran around the east end of the building... and there she was, in a classic, side on, one-handed stance, maybe twenty yards away. She fired twice, both slugs slammed into my chest, high up on the plate, and she turned and ran into the east end of the building. I barely felt the hits, and that made me wonder: *What the hell?*

And then I realized it was the suppressed twenty-two she was shooting, and that meant subsonic rounds, low velocity. She was also shooting left handed. Knowing all that, I felt a little better, but not much. If she hit me in the head, or clipped an artery, subsonic ammo or not, it would be all over. Anywhere else, even my unprotected legs, and I'd be okay…ish.

I ran after her, into the building. She was some twenty yards away, half-way up a flight of stairs. She turned and fired again, twice. One missed, the other hit my upper left arm; again the vest's sleeve took the hit, and I barely felt it. I let fly at her, five times, but she was already moving, low and fast. I missed.

She cleared the top of the stairs turned left and ran along the mezzanine. She stopped twice, and each time snapped off two shots. I fired back, once, twice, three times, four and then nothing, and she was away, running. I looked at the Glock; the slide was back. The damned thing was empty. *Shit!*

I ran up the stairs and chased after her along the mezzanine. I was at least thirty yards behind her when she slammed through double doors and was gone.

I followed her, but I went through the doors with a little more caution. I knew the Beretta 71 held eight rounds, but I'd lost count. I wasn't sure if she had one left or not.

I needn't have worried; she didn't. When I pushed through the doors, she was waiting for me.

"You all out, Harry?" she shouted. "I counted ten, and I'm betting you don't have a spare mag for that ankle piece. Me too."

She was standing in the middle of a vast open space that once must have been some sort of manufacturing area, but the room was empty; no machinery, not even an empty crate. She was perhaps thirty-five feet from where I was, breathing steadily, not in the least out of breath. Her right hand was at her side, blood dripping from her fingertips. In her left, she held what looked like a length of steel pipe.

"You up for it, Harry?" She hefted the pipe like it was a hammer. "If not, I'm out of here. We'll both live to continue this another day... and... you really, I mean really, don't look so good. What do you say?"

I looked at my legs, my left arm, both were still bleeding, but I'd seen worse. I flexed my left hand. It seemed to be working just fine. My chest? It felt like I'd swallowed a golf ball; not as bad as it was, but bad enough.

"You don't look so good yourself," I said, slowly stripping off my jacket and then the heavy vest.

"Oh, Harry. We don't have to do this. If I win, and I will, I'm gonna have to kill you."

I shook my head, "If we don't do it now," I replied, "I'll spend the rest of my days looking for you over my shoulder, and one of those days… you'll be there, right?"

She nodded, "A contract is a contract, and I have a reputation to protect. So be it!"

She walked slowly toward me. The steel pipe almost touching the floor.

I moved sideways, further into the room. As I did so, I had visions of scenes from the movie, Gladiator. Crazy? Yeah, I know.

Suddenly, she stepped quickly and lightly forward, on her toes, spun three-sixty while swinging backhanded with the pipe in a wide sweep. I was ready for it. I leaned back. The tip of the pipe swished past my face. I stepped quickly forward and… the sole of her left foot slammed into the back of my left arm with almost enough force to break it. Her foot hit right on the gash made by the shard of glass and the pain speared up my arm and, so it seemed, through my eyeballs and brain.

I staggered back. I figured she had me right then, but she seemed to be in no hurry.

She moved like a cat, circling me. I couldn't get near her, and judging by the mocking smile on her lips, she knew it. She moved in fast, struck and was gone again, out of range. I'd studied Grav Maga too, but this woman was an expert, far more skilled in the art than me. I was just an ex-cop.

She didn't dance, not at all like a boxer. Instead, she stalked me. She prowled, her arms and hands hanging loosely by her sides: the pipe in her left hand, blood still dripping from the fingers of her right hand, her head inclined slightly, her eyes half-closed, staring up at me through her lashes. Never once, not even for a second, did she take her eyes off mine. It was unnerving, and she seemed to be playing with me. *I have to end this quick. If I don't...*

"Harry, I really hate to do this, but you gave me no choice. Why didn't you just let it go? Another time, another place, we might have been friends."

I didn't even see it coming. One second she was in front of me, the next... no, not even the next second, she was that quick, she caught me with a glancing blow to the right thigh, then with another to my left ankle. She didn't need to kick. The pipe was working fine for her. I was aching all over. She was like quicksilver. She leaped in, swung the pipe, and was gone almost before I could react... and then it happened.

She came at me again, a blur of flying feet and steel pipe. She landed three blows in rapid succession: one to my left knee, one to my right forearm—I not only felt the bone snap, I heard it— and finally, she landed a good one just behind my left ear.

First, I experienced an instant white-hot pain in my arm, then it felt as if my brain had exploded. White lighting shot from back to front. They say when you're hit like that, your eyes glaze over. I never believed it, not until that moment. Everything became blurred. I couldn't see. My legs buckled. I dropped to my knees, then fell sideways. Unbelievably, I could still see her, dimly, a shadowy, wavering outline standing over me, her left hand holding the pipe high over her head. She was about to keep her promise and put me away, and there was nothing I could do about it. I was beaten, and I hadn't landed even a single blow.

I closed my eyes and waited for the final blow to fall, and I waited. Instead, I heard gunfire. I opened my eyes: nothing, just the ceiling, shimmering, like a mirage, high overhead. I turned my head, trying to see what was happening. Out of the corner of my eye, I could see someone standing just inside the doorway, feet together, arms outstretched. It was hardly a classic shooter's stance, but as I struggled to my elbows, pain lancing through my injured arm, I saw the gun drop from her fingers, and she ran toward me. I collapsed back onto the concrete floor, giving the back of my head another hefty clip.

She slipped her arms under my neck and pulled me to her, squeezing, and then I tasted the salt as the tears dripped onto my face. "How the hell did you find me?" I groaned.

"I didn't," Amanda whispered. "Tim did, thank God."

"Hey, Harry," I heard him say. "You don't look so good, Buddy."

I struggled to see him. He was standing behind her, looking down at me over her shoulder, his iPad clasped in both hands and, for once, he wasn't smiling. *That's not like him; not like him at all.*

"What about...?"

"She's dead," she whispered. "I shot the bitch... seven times..."

And before she could finish, I passed out.

When I came to just a few minutes later, I was surrounded by paramedics, the place was swarming with cops, and Kate was putting the cuffs on Amanda's wrists.

What the hell...?

And then I must have passed out again because I remember nothing more until...

Chapter 20
Tuesday, July 18, Morning

It was some thirty-six hours later when I woke up in the hospital. Amanda was at my bedside, so were August and Rose. They'd flown in from Puerto Rico in response to a phone call from Amanda.

The awaking was surreal, an almost out of body experience. I came to suddenly, in a flash of white light. I opened my eyes to find the room was quite dark. Just one overhead light shining in the far corner. No sooner had I rejoined the land of the living than two nurses bustled in and herded everyone out. Amanda, however, refused to go.

The next ten minutes saw a flurry of nurses in and out, some with carts—vital signs, EKG—one doctor, then another, until finally, one of them sat down beside the bed and asked me how I felt.

Now there's a stupid question. I felt like shit... My head was splitting. My eyeballs felt as if someone had put them through a nutcracker. My chest... the pain... no, it was more of a violent ache that permeated my entire upper torso, all the way through to my spine. My right arm was in a splint and throbbing... My legs... That's enough. You don't want to know the rest. And this clown was asking me how I felt. So I told him.

"I feel like shit. How do you think I feel?"

That didn't faze him one bit. Instead, he asked me another stupid question.

"On a scale of one to ten, with ten being the most severe, how would you describe the pain?"

I stared up at him, unable to believe what I was hearing. There I was, wrapped up like a damned Egyptian mummy, and he wanted to know how much I was hurting. I just looked at him and shook my head.

"I see. That bad, huh?" At least he sounded sympathetic. "Well, I can do something about that. I'll have one of the nurses fix you right up."

And he did. Bless him. Five minutes later, the pain had subsided, somewhat, and I was floating six inches above the bed. Well, that's what it felt like.

It seems I'd been in a coma since they'd brought me in. The blow to my head had resulted in a hairline fracture of the skull and severe concussion.

I don't remember much about the next several hours. I do vaguely remember being left alone with Amanda and my father and Rose, but that's about it.

I drifted in and out of consciousness throughout the night. August and Rose must have left sometime during the evening, but Amanda was still there the following morning when I awoke feeling... not great, but a whole lot better than I had.

I spent the next four days in the hospital, during which time several members of the local media came by, including Charlie Grove—Amanda sent them all on their way—and my staff were all over me, along with Kate and yes, even Lonnie.

It was another day before I was able to talk with any acuity... and by that I mean, able to talk without gibbering, and think rationally. Prior to that, I'm told, by none other than Tim, hell, he should know—that I babbled like a loon. So much for head injuries.

I was pleased to see and spend time with all of them, but sometimes it was like Grand Central Station in that room, and I tired quickly. When I did, Amanda shooed them all out.

It was toward the end of that second day that the conversation turned inevitably to what had happened. Up until then, I didn't even want to think about it. Every time I closed my eyes, and sometimes when they were wide open, I had vivid flashbacks, and the outcome was always the same; they ended with Kate clamping the cuffs on Amanda's wrists.

Finally, I asked her, "What the hell happened? How did you find me? I remember I took the batteries out of the phones. There was no way you could have followed me, us."

"I told you. It was Tim. Don't you remember?"

I shook my head, "No. Tell me."

"It was on Saturday, remember? When you told everyone they had to stay out of it."

I nodded.

"Well, Tim had me bug you, a GPS tracker. I attached it to your shoulder holster. You never go anywhere without it. So it was a no-brainer. But then we realized you can't wear that holster with a vest, so I bugged that too, your vest. It was easy. I made a small slit in the fabric inside the collar, and I slipped it inside. Even so, finding you wasn't easy. I had to wait for Tim to come and pick me up, and you know what a ditz he can be. Anyway, we did, we found you and… Well, it's over now. She's gone, and so is Harper."

"Amanda *you killed her*. You…"

She put a finger to my lips, "Shush. It's okay."

"But…"

"It's okay, Harry. It really is. At the time… well, I didn't even think. I just kept pulling the trigger…"

"I saw Kate," I said. "She was putting the cuffs on you. She arrested you."

She smiled, "No she didn't. The officers put those on me. You saw her taking them off."

"So what… what happened? Did they charge you?"

"No. They said she would have killed you, so deadly force was justified. No charges. Your

229

buddy, Larry Spruce, saw to that. He did interview me, though, but it was just a formality, maybe five minutes, no more than that."

****

Two days later they turned me loose from the hospital, and it was my turn to face the infamous Assistant District Attorney, Larry Spruce. By rights, being a friend, he should have recused himself but, as with Amanda, the interview was a formality. He did, however, make sure he had an assistant present to act as a witness. I asked August to attend, to represent me. Not that I needed an attorney, but what the hell, you never know, now do you? Well, as it turned out, I didn't, need an attorney.

It seems the only thing I could have been charged with was discharging a firearm in a public place, and I wasn't... charged.

It turned out that her name really was Calaway Jones. Surprise, surprise, and she was indeed ex-Mossad, another surprise... Not.

It also turned out that Interpol had been looking for her for more than two years. She was suspected of some fifteen assassinations all over Europe and the Middle East, but that was all it was: suspicion—no evidence. She was that good. They even searched her apartment in Paris, but they found nothing and, as Tim has said, she'd had almost zero Internet presence. She was indeed... a ghost.

That evening, when we got home, Amanda threw a party... Nah, not a party, just a little get together at the house, just for friends and family. Everyone had a good time, even me, although I was surely pleased to see them all leave, all except Kate and Bob. I asked them to stay for a while. Why? The truth was, I had Little Billy Harper on my mind. What the hell had happened? Who killed him? Who ordered it? I never did find out.

It was after ten o'clock when Kate and Bob drove away, and although I had my suspicions, I still had no answers. Oh, we talked about him, Harper, and Shady Tree, but I didn't ask Bob the question, not again. I'd believed him the first time he denied having anything to do with Harper's death. He'd never lied to me before, and I trusted him implicitly. No, my money was on Sergeant Lonnie Guest. I well-remembered the sly wink he'd given me, and I also remembered that he never actually denied it.

Amanda and me? I needed some time alone with her. Nope; not what you're thinking. I was still in no condition for that. I was still aching all over. No, I just wanted to be with her, talk to her, hold her hand, look at her, and I did.

It was a beautiful evening, and I was glad, no, I was grateful, to still be alive.

The End.

Thank you.

Thank you for taking the time to read Calaway Jones. If you enjoyed it, please consider telling your friends or posting a short review on Amazon (just a sentence will do). Word of mouth is an author's best friend and much appreciated. Thank you. Blair Howard.

Reviews are so very important. I don't have the backing of a major New York publisher. I can't afford to take out ads in magazines and on TV, but you can help get the word out.

To those many of my readers who have already posted reviews to this and my other novels, thank you for your past and continued support.

If you have comments or questions, you can contact me by email at blair@blairhoward.com, and you can visit my website http://www.blairhoward.com.

If you're new to the Harry Starke series, you might like to read the rest of the stories. They are available as individual eBooks, Paperbacks or Audiobooks. The first nine stories are also available in three Box Sets: Books 1-3, Books 4-

6, and Books 7-9, all at special reduced prices. Here are the links:

Box Set 1 US: http://amzn.to/294O6RF

Box Set 1 UK: http://amzn.to/2m80TJh

Box Set 2 US: http://amzn.to/2m7TMjM

Box Set 2 UK: http://amzn.to/2lK4NWc

Box Set 3 US: http://bit.ly/harrybooks7-9

Box Set 3 UK: http://bit.ly/harrybooks7-9UK